W9-CCT-239

Unwritten

UnwRittEn

TARA GILBOY

MANHASSET PUBLIC LIBRARY

JOLLY
FiSH
PRESS

Mendota Heights, Minnesota

[FANTASY]

J
Fic
Gilboy

Unwritten © 2018 by Tara Gilboy. All rights reserved. No part of this book may be used or reproduced in any manner whatsoever, including Internet usage, without written permission from Jolly Fish Press, except in the case of brief quotations embodied in critical articles and reviews.

First Edition
First Printing, 2018

Book design by Jake Slavik
Cover design by Jake Slavik
Cover illustration by Jomike Tejido

Jolly Fish Press, an imprint of North Star Editions, Inc.

This is a work of fiction. Names, characters, places, and incidents are either the product of the author's imagination or are used fictitiously, and any resemblance to actual persons living or dead, business establishments, events, or locales is entirely coincidental.

Library of Congress Cataloging-in-Publication Data
Names: Gilboy, Tara, author.
Title: Unwritten / Tara Gilboy.
Description: First edition. | Mendota Heights, Minnesota : Jolly Fish Press,
    [2018] | Summary: Twelve-year-old storybook character Gracie Freeman
    lives in the real world but longs to discover what happened in the story she
    came from.
Identifiers: LCCN 2018020898 (print) | LCCN 2018030936 (ebook) | ISBN
    9781631631788 (ebook) | ISBN 9781631631771 (pbk. : alk. paper)
Subjects: | CYAC: Characters in literature—Fiction. | Parent and
    child—Fiction. | Authors—Fiction. | Books and reading—Fiction. | LCGFT:
    Fantasy fiction. | Fiction.
Classification: LCC PZ7.1.G552 (ebook) | LCC PZ7.1.G552 Un 2018 (print) | DDC
    [Fic]—dc23
LC record available at https://lccn.loc.gov/2018020898

Jolly Fish Press
North Star Editions, Inc.
2297 Waters Drive
Mendota Heights, MN 55120
www.jollyfishpress.com

Printed in the United States of America

For Samantha, Julie, and Rita, who always believed in me

Always, for as long as she could recall, Gracie had the memory of fire.

It descended on her even now as she sat in her seventh-grade science class, swooping in out of nowhere as she hunched over her textbook. It wasn't a true memory—she'd never been in a fire, after all—but it felt real. The images came in flashes: the flicker of sparks, dark spots that moved, smokelike, lurking in the corners. Her skin burned hot, and she felt flushed.

"Story glimmers," Mom had explained. "Glimpses of things that would've happened if we hadn't escaped Bondoff. It doesn't matter what was written in that terrible book, it didn't come true. You're safe now. Just push the visions away—they're not real."

But Gracie rarely experienced a story glimmer this intensely, at least not when she was awake. Most of the time the glimmers were like spotting something out of the corner of her eye—the glare of flames reflected in a windowpane. Usually it was only in her dreams that she smelled the smoke, sensed the heat, and she found herself once again torn between curiosity and fear.

"Are you ill?" a voice said beside her.

Gracie turned. Walter watched her from behind glasses smudged with fingerprints because he was always shoving them up on his nose. He reminded Gracie of a plump owl.

"I'm fine." Gracie wiped sweat from her forehead and fought the irritation that always crept over her when she was around Walter. They had once been friends, when they were very young. That was nearly eight years ago now, but if Gracie looked closely, she could still make out the pearly outline of the scar beneath Walter's right eye where she had struck him.

Gracie was about to turn back to her homework when a red paper flyer slid from between the pages of Walter's book and fluttered to the floor. Gracie bent to pick it up and froze. Across the top, bold, black letters spelled the name "Gertrude Winters."

"Why do you have this?" The paper quivered in her fingers. Had Walter's parents finally told him the truth about the story, who they were?

Walter crooked his arm around the book he was reading. "I know I'm supposed to be reading the textbook," he said. "But I already finished the chapter yesterday, and I got this new book about dark matter last night. It's fascinating. Did you know—"

"Not the book. This." Gracie thrust the flyer onto his desk.

Walter turned it over in his hand and shrugged. "The woman at the bookstore stuck it in my bag. I've been using it as a bookmark."

"Are you going?"

"Where?"

"To see Gertrude Winters."

Walter blinked. "I don't read fiction. It's kind of a waste of time, don't you think? I read science books and—"

"Gertrude Winters is not a waste of time!" For a moment, Gracie had let herself hope that she'd have someone besides Mom to talk to about Gertrude Winters and the glimmers. "She's brilliant! She's—" Gracie's cheeks burned. The classroom was fading, replaced by the sharp snap of flames. The tang of smoke seared the back of her throat. Not now. She gripped the edge of her desk so tightly her knuckles turned white, willing the vision away. The glimmers were worse when her temper flared, and she counted silently to ten, which was what Mom told her to do when she was angry.

"You can have it"—Walter held the flyer out to her—"if you like this Winters person so much."

Gracie shoved the flyer into her folder.

"Are you sure you're not sick?" Walter said.

"It's just—" Gracie paused. "Do you ever feel funny, like you remember things that didn't really happen?"

Walter shrugged. "It's likely neurons misfiring in the brain and triggering the sensation of memory. That's how déjà vu works."

"Not déjà vu. More like—"

"Or it could be a sign of mental illness," Walter continued. "Or a vivid dream. Or—"

"Never mind." The bell rang, and, disappointed, Gracie gathered her books and hurried to lunch, leaving Walter mid-sentence.

✿

"You got this from Walter?"

Gracie sat at the kitchen table later that night. Her mother stood at the counter, clutching the flyer, one hip cocked, honey-colored curls tumbling around her shoulders. Her face wore the pinched, splotchy look that meant she was angry.

"Don't worry." Gracie pulled a thread from the tablecloth. "I didn't tell him anything."

"But why did he have it?"

"He said it came in a book he bought. Who cares why he had it? I think we should go see her."

Mom crumpled the flyer. "Absolutely not."

"I'm not saying we have to talk to her." Gracie stared at the flyer, wrinkled in Mom's fist. Mom had set her mouth in a hard line, and Gracie could feel her hopes slipping away. "It's the perfect opportunity to see her in person. She won't know who we are if we sit in the audience and listen."

"She might recognize us." Mom stuffed the flyer into the trashcan and thumped a jar of pickled eggs onto the counter.

"She wrote words; it's not like she has our photographs."

"And what if Cassandra's watching her, huh? Just watching and waiting to see if we try to contact Gertrude Winters? What if Cassandra was able to find us? I don't want to have anything to do with Gertrude Winters. I don't understand why you're so fascinated with her." Mom slammed pots around as she got the water boiling for potatoes. Mom always started banging things when she talked about Gertrude Winters.

"But—"

"I'm not going to discuss this anymore. It's for your own good."

Gracie blinked back tears of frustration. "Why can't we at least talk about it? You won't even listen to my side."

"You don't get a side in this. *I'm* the parent. I make the decisions."

"What I want matters, too!" The room grew hotter, a burned smell in the air. Gracie took a breath, balled the edge of the tablecloth in her fist, and focused on keeping her voice level as she said, "Aren't you even a *little* curious about what she wrote?"

"See? I knew you wanted to do more than listen. You want to talk to her."

"Don't you want to read our story?"

"Why would you want to read something so awful? I know more than enough already. You tell me what kind of a woman goes around killing children off?" Mom slashed her knife through a potato and dropped the pieces into the pot.

"Gertrude Winters didn't know. She thought she was just writing a story."

Mom snorted. "Is that supposed to make it any better? Besides, I have to work on Saturday."

"You could at least let *me* see her if you don't want to."

"No." Mom turned her back to Gracie and opened the freezer. "Do you want peas or corn with dinner?"

But Gracie was already gone, halfway to her bedroom, where she slammed the door with a satisfying thud.

2

That night, Gracie dreamed of fire, hot and crackling. There was rage too, but mostly smoke and flames and a woman with long black hair and a crown atop her head that glinted in the firelight. Gracie had the dream so often that it no longer frightened her, and it wasn't the nightmare but the sound of Mom's screams that finally woke her. Gracie wasn't the only one with story glimmers.

Gracie padded to Mom's room. The moonlight sent shadows skittering over the walls. Mom moaned and clutched the pillow. "Jacob," she said. "Gracie." Instead of shaking her awake, Gracie sat on the floor cross-legged and waited. Whenever Mom dreamed of this Jacob-person, Gracie simply listened, hoping Mom would say something more, some clue, but she was always disappointed. Tonight was no different. After muttering the names one last time, Mom grew quiet, though her fingers still kneaded the blankets, and a line puckered between her eyebrows.

The room was cold, and Gracie tucked her nightgown over her bare legs, still sweaty from her dream, the floorboards creaking beneath her.

Mom's eyes snapped open. "What are you doing in here? Did you have a nightmare again?"

Gracie nodded, and Mom patted the mattress beside her. Gracie climbed into bed. The sheets smelled of laundry soap and Mom's shampoo.

"Was I talking in my sleep?" Mom said.

"No," Gracie said. "You didn't say a word."

She wasn't sure why she lied, whether she was trying not to upset Mom or whether she just wanted to keep secrets from her, the way Mom kept them from Gracie. She'd long suspected "Jacob" was her father's name, and by keeping it to herself, it remained her own private gem she held inside, rolling the sound of it in her mouth like a marble. Jacob.

Mom smoothed Gracie's hair. "I'm sorry we fought earlier."

Mom's face looked so sad in the moonlight that Gracie found her anger cooling. A part of Gracie wanted to do nothing more than curl up next to her in bed and sleep, like she'd done when she was a little girl. Life would be so much simpler if she could forget about Gertrude Winters the way Mom wanted her to, but the other part of Gracie knew that was impossible.

"I'm sorry too," she said.

"You know I only want what's best for you."

The anger prickled again, but Gracie shoved it down. She took a deep breath and chose her words carefully. "I don't understand why you think it's best for me not to know what she wrote. I want to know who I am."

"Because it doesn't matter what she wrote," Mom said. "You're Gracie, my daughter. You can be whoever you want to be."

"If you'd just tell me a little more—"

"Why can't you let the past be the past?" There was a catch in Mom's voice, and Gracie shifted under the blanket, her stomach clenching. She felt terribly guilty when Mom cried, and it seemed like tears always followed when Gracie asked about Bondoff, the land in the story where Gracie was born. She wanted to apologize, but somehow the words wouldn't come out. How could she be sorry for wanting to know who she was, where she came from?

Soon soft snores signaled Mom was asleep, but Gracie lay awake for a long time, staring at the ceiling. Mom acted like it was so simple, but it wasn't. How could she let the past be the past when she was reminded of it every day? There were the story glimmers, the nightmares, and Mom's constant worry. Gracie had grown up fearing Queen Cassandra the way other children dreaded the Boogeyman or monsters under the bed.

The nightmares started when Gracie was four years old, not long after she hit Walter. She'd wakened almost every night, shrieking and kicking, the bed sheets twisting around her sweaty legs. Always Mom rushed in and stroked her hair and tried to soothe her, but for the longest time, Mom hadn't explained the dreams to Gracie.

In the dreams, there was always fire and rage and the woman with the crown, beckoning to Gracie through the flames. Sometimes Gracie wanted to go to the woman, but then fear washed over her, pinning her in place. The woman was starkly beautiful, but something threatening lurked about her too, the haughty slash of eyebrows against pale skin, the sharp angles of her cheekbones.

After many months of this, when Gracie had grown so terrorized by the dreams that she refused to go to bed and stayed up until the wee hours of the morning, when she'd grown thin and pale from lack of sleep, Mom had told her the truth. Or a version of it.

"The dreams are glimmers," Mom said. "Like a special kind of memory. We're not ordinary people. A long time ago, a woman named Gertrude Winters wrote a story about us. You were supposed to die in the story, but I took you out of it and into the outside world when you were a tiny baby, so you would be safe. The glimmers are visions of things that would have happened in the story if we'd stayed. But there's nothing to be afraid of here; nothing can hurt you anymore."

Gracie touched the smooth freckled skin of her arms, her tangled brown hair, then the row of fairy tales lining the bookshelf beside her bed. "Am I a princess in the story?"

Mom's face tightened, and she busied herself plumping Gracie's pillows. "You can be whoever you want to be."

"I want to be a princess." Gracie liked this idea. She wiped her nose on her pajama sleeve. "Who's the pretty lady in my dream?"

The hand on the pillow froze. For a fraction of a second, Mom's eyes bored into hers, but she leaned quickly to kiss Gracie on the forehead, and when she pulled away again, her face had relaxed once more. "A very bad person named Queen Cassandra. She's the one we're hiding from. We'll never let her find us—I promise."

"She wants me to die?"

Mom crawled into bed beside her, so their heads rested together on the pillow. "It doesn't matter what she wants—I won't let her get you."

"What about Walter? He dreamed about her too."

"Walter told you that?"

Gracie nodded.

Mom pulled the sheets tight around them both. She was silent so long Gracie thought she'd fallen asleep, but finally Mom said, "Walter's from our story too. His parents don't want him to know, so you can't tell him. He's not as brave as you; they think it would scare him."

"He isn't brave. He cried when I hit him."

"You shouldn't have hit him; that was bad."

Gracie smiled. "I don't like Walter. And I don't want to tell him anything. He's bossy all the time. And he picks his nose. I saw him."

"It'll be our secret then."

Now, as Gracie lay in her mother's bed, she wondered if Mom regretted telling her. Perhaps she wished she'd kept it a secret, the way Walter's parents had. Certainly, Mom didn't like answering questions about Bondoff, nor was she pleased when Gracie tried to answer them for herself. When Gracie was eight, she'd tried to find a copy of the story at the library, and when the librarian mentioned it to Mom, Mom wouldn't take her back to the library for a year. The search had been useless anyway. Apparently

Gertrude Winters never published the story about Gracie, and last year Gracie had gotten grounded for a month when Mom caught her writing a letter to Gertrude Winters asking her about it. But now, Gertrude Winters was going to be nearby, in person. And as Gracie watched Mom sleep, she knew she couldn't let Mom deter her any longer. She was tired of secrets. She was going to that bookstore to see Gertrude Winters.

3

On Saturdays, Mom worked a double shift waitressing at a diner—the tips were good on weekends—so when Gracie woke up Saturday morning, Mom was already rushing out the door.

"I left your breakfast on the stove." Mom planted a kiss on Gracie's forehead as she searched for her keys. "What are your plans for today?"

"I might go for a bike ride." Gracie avoided looking at Mom as she pulled a plate from the cupboard. Now that her anger had faded, she felt bad for lying.

"Stay off the busy streets," Mom said. "I'll bring pizza home for dinner."

Mom hated pizza, so Gracie knew this was a peace offering. Mom liked the kinds of foods she'd eaten in Bondoff. Foods like the apples fried in butter she'd left for Gracie's breakfast, or cabbage soup and ginger cakes. Rarely did she make things normal families ate, like cheeseburgers and pizza, so Gracie figured this was meant as an apology for not allowing Gracie to see Gertrude Winters. The guilt pricked more deeply, but seeing Gertrude Winters was too important to let that deter her.

"You don't have to get pizza." Gracie popped an apple slice into her mouth and licked butter and cinnamon from her fingers. "We could have porridge if you'd like that better."

Mom pressed the back of her hand to Gracie's forehead. "Are you feeling okay?"

"Ha ha." Gracie swatted her hand away. She watched from the window as Mom started the car and backed out of the driveway. When she was sure Mom was really gone, she scurried into Mom's room, her heart pounding. Today she was going to meet Gertrude Winters!

Mom kept an old-fashioned steamer trunk at the foot of her bed. Inside, she stored her most important possessions. Mostly these included photos of Gracie as a baby, a lock of Gracie's hair from her first haircut, drawings Gracie made in kindergarten, Mother's Day cards and pebbles Gracie had collected, and other souvenirs of the small things she and Mom had done together. But Gracie wasn't interested in these as she knelt beside the trunk, glancing guiltily over her shoulder. Mom had never expressly forbid her from going through her things. Still, she couldn't help feeling that she was betraying her in some small way, invading her privacy. But she pushed the thought from her mind as she sifted past Mom's mementos until she found the large lockbox at the bottom.

She had no trouble with the lock—she'd watched Mom open it before and taken note of the combination, which was easy to remember: the date, month, and year that Mom had fled with

Gracie, taken her out of their story and into the outside world. It was the date she'd saved Gracie's life. As Gracie turned the knobs, the lock clicked and the latch sprung open. She peeked over her shoulder and listened once again to make sure she didn't hear Mom coming home before lifting the lockbox lid.

Inside the lockbox were the clothes they'd been wearing the day they left their story. Mom's long wool dress, the cloth rough and itchy; a shawl; Gracie's lighter cotton nightgown and bonnet, so tiny—Gracie was not even a year old when they left. She ran her fingers over the cloth, lifted the shawl to her nose to see if it still contained any of the scents of the place she came from, but all it smelled like was the inside of the trunk mixed with something not unlike the smell of a wet wool scarf wrapped around her face in winter, when snow stuck to it and melted under her hot breath.

Gracie set the clothes aside. The most important item in the trunk was only a blank rectangle of paper, jagged on one edge, as if it had been torn from a book. Mom had shown it to her a couple years ago, when Gracie had questioned the truth of the story about where they came from. It wasn't usual, everyday paper—parchment, Mom called it, which she said was a kind of paper made of animal skin. And it felt like skin too; even now, it was warm, as if recently held in someone's hand. There was something special about the parchment—it was how Mom had taken Gracie out of the story and into the outside world, though she refused to tell Gracie how it worked.

"It's too dangerous," Mom had said. "And not something you need to know. It's not like we're ever going back. We're staying right here where we're safe and sound and free of Queen Cassandra."

Gracie rubbed the parchment between her fingers. It was soft and pliable, and it seemed to grow warmer the longer she held it, as if absorbing the heat from her skin. She could almost sense it whispering to her—not words, just a sound like the wind or the faint rustle of pages turning.

Mom thought everything was dangerous.

Gracie would put the parchment back before Mom came home from work. Perhaps Gertrude Winters would be able to tell her something about it. Not that she planned on asking—she hadn't lied when she told Mom she would sit in the audience and listen. But what if the author recognized Gracie? Gracie might need the parchment to prove who she really was. Perhaps they'd become friends, and Gertrude Winters could tell her all about her story.

Something about the parchment's warmth pulled on Gracie, making her eyelids heavy, but she shook the feeling away. She folded the parchment and placed it in her pocket. It was time to meet Gertrude Winters.

〜〜

Everything looked so ordinary that Gracie could scarcely believe she was in the right place. Her blood pumped so furiously she felt as if she had a marching band between her ears, and yet the bookstore was quiet, with people browsing at shelves or reading silently at tables. The only sign that Gracie's life was about to change was a poster in the window that displayed a headshot of

Gertrude Winters and the title of her new book, which the poster called "an elegant *tour de force* about family secrets." Gracie had never been to see an author speak before, had never even met an author; she supposed she'd been expecting crowds and streamers, something a bit more flashy. Gracie went to the counter, and the cashier looked up.

"I'm here to see Gertrude Winters," Gracie said.

The girl snapped her gum. "In the back room. Over by the bathrooms." She jerked her thumb toward the restroom sign. Gracie made her way toward it, past the literature section and the children's area until she spotted a little room next to the science section where a dozen people sat on folding chairs. None of them were Gertrude Winters. A card table had been set up at the back of the room, where a bald man sold Gertrude Winters's books. Gracie took a seat in the front row. There were still five minutes before it was supposed to start. She had brought thirty dollars, all she had saved. Should she buy a book now? But she wanted Winters to sign it—maybe she should wait until Winters arrived. She wasn't sure how these things worked. And she didn't want to lose her place in front by getting up to buy a book.

A murmur rose behind her, and a small gray-haired woman ambled to the front of the room. The bald man selling books dashed to the podium and whispered to her, and the woman waved him away. Was this Gertrude Winters? She certainly appeared older than in her pictures on the book jackets and the poster. But, yes, it must be her. She unloaded papers from a tote bag and arranged them on the podium. She wore a blue skirt and blazer, and her glasses were attached to a silver chain looped around her neck. She looked like a schoolteacher. Gracie's palms were sweaty, and she wiped them on her jeans. Her mouth felt dry. She was close enough to touch her, to speak to her. But what could she say? *Hello, I'm Gracie. Do you remember writing about me?*

Gertrude Winters glanced up and caught Gracie staring. Gracie looked away quickly. "It's not often I have young people at my events," Gertrude Winters said. "Are you here with your mother?"

Gracie shook her head. Gertrude Winters had spoken to her! She tried to think of something clever to say, but all she could manage was "I really like your books."

Gertrude Winters smiled and turned back to her papers.

The next half hour passed in a haze; Gracie was so excited to actually be in the writer's presence that she had a hard time focusing on what she said. The man from the bookstore introduced her, talked about her writing and her work as a college professor who studied fairy tales. He called her new book a "gothic romance that blends fact and fairy tale to create something dangerous and new." Then Gertrude Winters talked about her new book and her writing process.

"I have always been fascinated with the darkness inside people," Gertrude Winters said. "We are not all good and bad, and sometimes the villains can be the most fascinating characters."

Gracie wished Gertrude wouldn't ramble on about villains and would instead say something about Gracie's story, but she still loved hearing Winters's voice, loved hearing her read aloud from her new book. The words blurred into one another, lulling her. She touched the parchment in her pocket. She felt calm, no longer bothered by story glimmers, happy to be right where she was, in this room with Gertrude Winters. Too soon it was over, and Gertrude had closed her book and asked the audience for questions.

"Where do you get your ideas?" one woman asked.

"Mostly from the world around me," Gertrude Winters said. "From things I see, people I know. I like to think all my characters are based on myself, at least a little bit. The good and the bad."

Before Gracie could stop herself, her hand was in the air. She had to know. "Do you ever feel like your stories are real?" she asked.

Gertrude Winters pressed a finger to her lips. "That's a good question," she said. "Let me ask you something: if stories, or the characters in them, live in the minds of readers, then doesn't that mean they exist in some dimension? I've written a good many characters who felt much more real to me than some of the dull people I've known. Certainly, I think stories and characters are real to the people who love them."

This wasn't exactly the answer Gracie had been looking for, but she pushed on. "Do you have a favorite character?"

Gertrude Winters shook her head. "I could never pick a favorite. Though I do love Anna from my new book."

"What about a favorite story?" Gracie said.

Gertrude Winters smiled. "My favorite story is always the one I am currently working on."

Gertrude Winters turned to call on someone else, but Gracie thrust her hand back into the air, rising slightly off her seat, before she lost her courage.

"Do you have any stories you wrote that you haven't published?" Gracie said.

Winters nodded. "Many. Some I wrote for fun; some I tried to sell to publishers and couldn't."

"What are they about?"

Gertrude Winters smiled. "If I tried to tell you all that, we would run out of time. Let's give someone else a turn to ask a question, shall we?" And she nodded to a lady with an ugly green handbag who asked something stupid about research, and Gracie slumped in her chair.

ରଝ

Gertrude Winters was signing books afterward, and Gracie knew her time was running short. So far, Winters hadn't said anything useful that could give Gracie a clue to her story, and she knew she couldn't let the author leave without finding out what she'd written about her.

Gracie bought a book from the balding man and got in line to have Gertrude Winters sign it. She watched the author's hands move over the paper as she signed books for the people ahead of Gracie in line. Winters's hands were small, the nails short and rounded, and she had a callous on her middle finger. These were the hands that had written Gracie's story. When it was Gracie's turn, Winters took her book and smiled at her. She had a pen stuck behind one ear, another in her hand. "Ah," Winters said. "The girl with so many questions. It's always nice to have young readers. Who should I make it out to?"

"Gracie." She studied Winters's face for any sign of recognition, but the author only nodded and clicked her pen, as if Gracie was simply another fan.

Gertrude Winters signed the book and passed it back to her. She started to turn to the next person in line. Gracie was about to lose her chance. Her feet slid forward, then stopped.

"Bondoff," Gracie blurted.

"What?" Gertrude Winters said.

"You wrote a story about a place called Bondoff, right?"

"How do you know that?"

"Can you tell me what happens in the story?" Gracie bent over the table, so her face was level with Winters's.

The author leaned back, her hand going to the pearls at her throat. "That story was a disaster. I never published it. Who have you been talking to?"

"It has a character named Gracie, right?"

Winters narrowed her eyes, studying her. She tapped her pen against her lip.

"What's Gracie like?" Gracie said.

"I don't remember," Gertrude Winters said. "It was so long ago. I didn't like the story, so I threw it away."

The balding man pressed Gracie forward. "Sorry," he said. "There are a lot more people to get to. We've got to keep the line moving." And just like that, Gracie lost her chance.

4

Gracie pressed the book to her chest, feeling like she might cry as she left the back room. She'd been so close, and yet somehow managed to let it all slip between her fingers. She hadn't gotten any answers. She'd seen Gertrude Winters, in person, and still had no idea what Winters had written about her.

"Gracie?"

Gracie's head snapped up. Walter stood in the science section next to the restroom sign, holding a stack of books. He wore a backpack covered in buttons with various slogans on them. One said "I ♥ Science." Another said: "Never trust an atom: they make up everything."

"What are you doing here?"

"I finished my dark matter book and wanted to get another one." Walter held a book out, thumbing to the middle and jabbing at a picture of outer space. "Did you know there is so much dark matter in the universe that we can't see that scientists think it proves there are other dimensions?"

Gracie shrugged. Didn't he realize she was in the middle of a crisis? "That's nice."

Walter closed the book and slid it back onto the shelf. "Did you get to meet that author you were talking about?"

"Barely." Gracie bit her lip. "There was a line."

"That's too bad." Walter tilted his head. "Is that one of her books?"

Gracie looked down at the book in her hands. She'd almost forgotten she had it. "Yes. She signed it." She'd have to hide the book when she got home. If Mom found an autographed copy of a Gertrude Winters novel, she'd freak out.

"Can I see it?"

"I thought you didn't like fiction?" Gracie had meant to be sarcastic, but Walter only shrugged. She passed him the book, and Walter flipped to the inscription. The back room had nearly emptied. Soon Gertrude Winters would be gone. She was packing up her things and placing them in her tote bag. She stood and walked toward Gracie. Was she coming to talk to her after all? But no, she strolled right past her and into the bathroom.

"That's Gertrude Winters," Gracie said.

"She's old," Walter said.

"It's funny to think of her having to pee like a normal person." Gracie was getting an idea.

"Where are you going?"

"I'll be right back," Gracie said. And she followed Gertrude Winters into the bathroom.

≈≈≈

Gracie paced in front of the mirror, waiting for Gertrude Winters to come out of her stall. She caught a glimpse of herself and was startled by the wild look in her eyes. She had to calm down or Gertrude Winters was going to think she was crazy. Maybe she was crazy. After all, she'd stalked an author into the bathroom. Gracie smoothed her hair. She splashed water on her face. What was taking so long? Gracie probably shouldn't question her while she was still in her stall; she might get mad. And then Gertrude Winters came out and washed her hands at the other sink. She smiled at Gracie in the mirror.

"Please," Gracie blurted out. "Tell me anything you remember about your Bondoff story. Tell me about Gracie."

Gertrude Winters slowly dried her hands on a paper towel. "Why are you so fascinated with that story? How do you even know about it?"

"I can't tell you," Gracie said. "But it's important."

"Like I said, I don't remember much about it. It was a kind of fairy tale, a novel I wrote for adults. It didn't work very well, so I threw away the draft and wrote something new."

Gracie caught Gertrude Winters by the sleeve. "Please, you have to try to remember more than that. I need to know—"

Gertrude Winters was looking past Gracie now, over her shoulder at the door, as if trying to think of some way to escape. "I have to go. I'm running late."

Gracie gripped her sleeve tighter. "Please, I need to know. I'm—" Gracie took a deep breath. "I'm Gracie. From the story. I know it sounds crazy, but my mom took me out of the story so I wouldn't die, and you can't tell anyone because then Queen Cassandra could find me. But please tell me what happens in the story. Am I a princess? Who is my father?"

Gertrude Winters placed a hand on Gracie's shoulder. Her eyebrows knitted together in worry and something like pity. "You don't look well. Maybe we should find your parents. Is there someone you would like me to call for you?"

"No!" Gracie threw off Winters's hand and dug the parchment from her pocket. "I can prove it! My mom brought this from the story. It's magic; it's how we got out of the story! See?" She shoved the paper into Gertrude Winters's hand. Surely she would sense the parchment's power the way Gracie had, would remember having written about it. She'd believe Gracie now.

Gertrude Winters unfolded the parchment. She took the pen from behind her ear. "Would you like another autograph?" she said.

"No, I want you to tell me—"

But Gertrude Winters had already flattened the parchment on the counter. She scrawled her name across it in thick black strokes and held it out to Gracie. Gracie and Gertrude both watched as the ink seeped into the paper. The parchment shimmered like a hologram before disappearing altogether. For one startled moment, the author's eyes met Gracie's. And then Gertrude Winters faded away just as quickly, her body dissolving like a wisp of smoke.

5

Gracie stared at the spot where Gertrude Winters had stood, moments before. What had happened? Gertrude Winters had written her name on the parchment. Then the words had disappeared, the parchment in Winters's hand vanishing along with them. Then Winters herself had faded, her body growing ghostlike, like a mirage, until she was gone too. Mom had warned her the parchment was dangerous, but Gracie didn't know it could do that!

Gracie sank to the ground, feeling hot then cold, the way she did when she had a bad sunburn. Her hands shook. Where had Gertrude Winters gone? She hadn't disappeared forever, had she?

Gracie peeked in the stalls, half-hoping to find Gertrude Winters crouched in one, playing a trick on her. But no. Gracie eased the bathroom door open. She wanted nothing more than to rush home and climb into bed and sleep and find this was all a bad dream.

"Hey, don't leave your book!"

Gracie had forgotten Walter. He stood beside the science shelves, holding out the book Gertrude Winters had signed.

"Did you talk to her?" Walter's face was hopeful.

Gracie shook her head, wishing Mom had not forbidden her from discussing the story with Walter. "Do me a favor: Don't tell your parents you saw me here, all right?"

"Why?" Walter hitched his backpack higher on his shoulders.

"I'm grounded. I wasn't supposed to leave the house today." The lie came quickly to her lips.

Walter nodded. Gracie peeked over her shoulder at the back room, where the bald man waited beside Gertrude Winters's tote bag. He glanced toward the bathroom. Gracie scurried from the store, hoping to be far away by the time anyone noticed Gertrude Winters was missing.

᠅

When Gracie got home, she was relieved to find Mom hadn't gotten off work early. She had no choice but to confess—Mom must know how to bring Gertrude Winters back—but Gracie needed some time to think about how to tell her. Unless . . . Perhaps Winters would reappear, and it would all turn out to be some kind of trick. Or maybe the parchment's magic would wear off, and everything would return to normal again. And why did Gertrude Winters have to write her name on the parchment anyway? Gracie hadn't asked her for another autograph. If you really thought about it, this was all Gertrude Winters's fault for writing her name on other people's things without being invited.

Gracie sat in the living room with the television turned off, her heart quickening every time she heard a car drive by. Any minute now, Mom's car would pull into the driveway, and Gracie would have to tell her what she'd done. It wasn't so much that she feared Mom's anger—Mom would forgive her—but telling her would make it real, would make it true that Gertrude Winters had really disappeared. Mom was always frightened about something, always reluctant to talk about the story and Gertrude Winters, and for the first time, Gracie started to consider that Mom's fears might be justified. When Gracie's phone rang, she jumped. But the voice on the other end wasn't Mom. It was Walter.

"Hey, was that author lady in the bathroom when you were?"

"Why?"

"Things got weird after you left the bookstore today," Walter said.

"What do you mean 'weird'?" Gracie tried to keep the fear out of her voice.

"That author lady never came out of the bathroom. The people at the bookstore were looking all over for her."

"You didn't tell anybody you saw me, did you?" Gracie's hand tightened on the phone.

"No, but I don't like lying! They asked me if I'd seen her. I told them I saw her go in but not come out, and they asked me if anybody else had gone in, and I said no."

Gracie closed her eyes. "Thanks for not telling on me."

"Did you see her in there?"

"She was going to the bathroom. I don't look in people's stalls when they're going to the bathroom."

"So you didn't notice anything strange?"

"She probably came out and you didn't see her. She probably had somewhere to be." Gracie wrapped a strand of hair around her finger and pulled until it hurt.

"But she left all her stuff at the bookstore. That's what the clerk said. She left her bag with her wallet, even."

"She's old. Maybe she forgot them. People don't just disappear, Walter."

"I guess. I thought if you saw anything suspicious you could tell the people at the bookstore."

"I have to go—my mom's calling me. I'll talk to you later, okay?" Gracie hung up the phone and rested her head on her elbows. So Gertrude Winters was really missing. Gracie couldn't pretend it hadn't happened. She was so lost in her own thoughts, she didn't hear Mom come home until the keys were already jangling in the door. Mom walked in carrying a pizza box. "I got pepperoni!" she said.

๛

Gracie pretended to be sick all night and the next day. She didn't eat any of the pizza Mom brought home, and she lay in bed with her eyes closed all the next day, faking sleep and listening to the rain patter on the roof. She had to confess sometime, before Mom went into her trunk and discovered the parchment missing. Mom always said honesty was the best policy; but if *she* had been honest, rather than secretive, she would have told Gracie not to take the parchment because it could make people disappear. Then none of this would have happened. Gracie was frightened of what Mom would say when Gracie told her. Could the two of them disappear too? Every so often, Mom came into Gracie's room and pressed the back of her hand to Gracie's forehead. "You don't have a fever," she said.

Around suppertime, she made Gracie get out of bed and come into the living room. "It may do you good to sit up and eat something. I cooked soup. Exactly the thing for a stormy day."

Gracie sat on the couch under a blanket, sipping at the chicken broth Mom handed her. It had little flecks of rice and turnip in it, one of the Bondoff recipes Mom liked so much. Gracie's stomach hurt. Perhaps she really was getting sick.

Mom flipped on the television. The evening news was on, and Gracie froze when a picture of Gertrude Winters flashed onto the screen. "In local news," the anchorman said, "yesterday renowned author Gertrude Winters disappeared from an event at a local bookstore." Mom turned the volume up. Gracie ducked her head and pulled at a hangnail. The rain had picked up, and tree branches rattled against the window. "Police are investigating her whereabouts, but there are no signs foul play was involved. If you have any information—"

"See!" Mom sank onto the couch beside Gracie, her expression bordering on triumphant. "I told you it was a good thing you didn't go see Gertrude Winters!"

Gracie swallowed hard. "What do you think happened to her?"

"Who knows? But a horrible woman like that? Think how many people must have it out for her."

"You don't know she's a horrible woman," Gracie said.

"Well, she certainly writes nasty things. It's a sick mind that kills children off."

Gracie set her soup on the coffee table. "Mom," she started, but before she could finish her sentence, the doorbell rang.

Mom stood to answer it, and Gracie pulled the blanket around her shoulders. Who would be venturing into the storm at this hour? What if it was the police? Had Gracie been spotted in the bathroom with Winters after all?

But when the door swung open, only Walter and his parents stood on the front stoop, damp from the storm, Walter looking confused, his parents indignant. "We need to talk," Walter's mother said.

6

"Walter told us something very interesting," Walter's dad said. His name was Thomas, and he looked like an older version of Walter, but with rounder glasses and hair that was graying at the edges. He sat on the couch beside his wife, Audrey, a plump, blonde woman who slid over and made room for Walter between them. None of them looked at Gracie. Gracie tried to catch Walter's eye, but he seemed fascinated by a loose thread on the cuff of his shirtsleeve.

"Go on," Audrey said, nudging Walter. "Tell Gracie's mother what you told us."

Walter shook his head, and Audrey placed her hand on his knee. Her nails were painted a shiny lacquered red. "Tell her," she said, an edge in her voice now.

Walter finally looked up and met Gracie's eyes. "I'm sorry, Gracie," he said. "I didn't want to tell, but she's *missing*. It was on the news."

Gracie took deep breaths and tried to fight the anger sweeping over her. The room was fading, the voices a distant lull as Walter's parents repeated how Walter had seen Gracie at the bookstore, how she had been with Gertrude Winters. They all seemed far away, removed from her. In her mind's eye, Gracie saw a smoky tunnel, the woman with the crown at the end of it. Queen Cassandra. Beneath her crown, she wore a black veil that flapped around her shoulders. She crooked a finger at Gracie. Come. Gracie would step toward her, but flames blocked the way. It was Walter's fault. And then Gracie was pulled back to reality with the pressure of Mom's hand on her shoulder. "Is this true?" Mom said.

Before Gracie could answer, the doorbell rang again. Mom sprang from the couch, her muscles tense, but Thomas flicked his hand dismissively. "That'll be Jacob," he said.

"You called Jacob?" Mom's voice was tight, her body rigid. Despite Gracie's worry about being caught, she was immediately alert for talk about Jacob. Was she really going to see him in person? For so long he'd been only a name. Gracie had assumed he was still in Bondoff—if he was her father, that is.

"I invited him here," Thomas said. "He needed to know, too. We're all going to have to deal with this together."

"You invited him to *my* house?" Mom said.

"Oh for Pete's sake, someone needs to get the door." Audrey clomped to the door and let in a tall, bearded man in jeans and a coffee-colored flannel shirt. His hair was wet with rain and reminded Gracie of soggy leaves. He stood awkwardly in the entryway, his hands jammed in his pockets. "Hello, Elizabeth," he said, his eyes finding Mom.

Mom sank onto the cushion beside Gracie. "You may as well sit down," she said briskly. "And try not to drip all over the floor."

Jacob wiped his feet carefully on the rug and perched on the edge of couch. He stared at his boots; wet grass clung to the soles. Every so often he glanced at Gracie. His eyes were the same greenish-gray as hers, and he hunched his shoulders forward, the same way she did when she was nervous. Mom sat angled away from him, her lips pressed together so tightly they seemed to disappear inside her mouth.

"Gracie was about to tell us what happened yesterday," Thomas said.

"Walter, why don't you go wait in the car until we're done here?" Audrey said.

Mom clutched Gracie's hand. "So you're going to accuse *my daughter* of things, but still try to protect your son from knowing anything?"

"I think we can see from what happened yesterday what a mistake it was to tell Gracie anything! She went seeking out Gertrude Winters!"

"Walter and Gracie were both at that bookstore!" Mom said. "Leaving Walter in the dark didn't keep him away from Gertrude Winters, did it? Maybe you don't have as much control as you would like to think."

"Walter, the car, now!" Audrey tapped his knee with one of her blood-red fingernails.

"I don't want to—"

"Let him wait in Gracie's room," Mom said. "No need to send him out in the rain."

Walter trudged off to Gracie's room followed by Audrey, who closed the door behind him before returning to the living room.

Mom squeezed Gracie's hand. "Now tell us what happened," she said quietly. "Don't be afraid. I'm sure it's not as bad as they're making it out to be."

Gracie took a deep breath. Everyone's eyes were on her, accusing.

"I went to see Gertrude Winters speak," Gracie said. "I just wanted to listen to her talk, I swear. But after the book signing, I ran into her in the bathroom."

"*Followed* her into the bathroom," Audrey said.

Gracie bit her lip but ignored the interruption. "In the bathroom, I showed her the parchment." Mom sucked in her breath sharply. Gracie closed her eyes. "I didn't mean for her to do anything to it. But she thought I wanted an autograph. She signed the paper. And then she disappeared."

All this time, Jacob had remained silent, but now he stood and paced, rubbing his chin. "So that's it," he said quietly. "Gertrude Winters is in Bondoff."

Mom threw up her hands, but Gracie turned to Jacob; there was something reassuring about his broad chest and scruffy beard, the calm way he spoke. Mom was never so forthcoming about the story world, and Jacob hadn't scolded Gracie for what she'd done either. She wondered what kind of father Jacob would be. "That's where she went?"

Jacob ran his hand through his shaggy hair. "The parchment is a portal between the story world and the real world. If Gertrude disappeared, it's because she went inside."

"So how do we get her back?" Gracie asked.

"We don't," Thomas said.

"We can't leave her!" Gracie said.

"The only way to rescue her would be to go get her ourselves," Jacob pulled the curtain aside and peered out into the storm. "I still have my piece of the parchment. I could go look for her and bring her back."

"It's too dangerous," Mom said. "What if Cassandra saw you there?"

"Besides," Audrey added, "Gertrude Winters still has Elizabeth's parchment. She may figure out how to get back out of the story on her own."

"And if not," Mom said, "she created Cassandra and Bondoff. Let her rot in the world she created."

"It's not that simple, though." Jacob closed the curtain and turned to face them. "Cassandra is bound to find Gertrude Winters in the story world. She'll take the parchment back and then she'll ask her where she came from. Gertrude Winters can tell her about Gracie and the book signing. She can tell her the name of our town. It's only a matter of time before Cassandra shows up here."

Mom stared at the ceiling, her lips pressed together as if thinking hard. "Then we've got to leave," she said. "Tonight."

Audrey laughed shrilly. "Where are we supposed to go?"

"We can all go to my house first," Jacob said. "I have a trailer out in the woods. I don't have an address—I'm completely off the grid. It would be hard for Cassandra to find us there. Once we're safe there, we can decide what to do next."

"We'll need to pack some things." Thomas stood.

"We should get the kids out of here right away." Mom rubbed Gracie's shoulder as if trying to warm her, though the room wasn't cold.

"I can take them now," Jacob said. "And you three can pack and follow me when you're done."

"I don't like the idea of sending Walter off with Gracie." Audrey crossed her arms over her chest. "You don't know—"

"I agree with Jacob," Thomas said. "I think it's our only option. Elizabeth can follow us in her car since I know the way."

Gracie turned to Mom. "You're not going to send me off with a stranger."

But Mom ignored Gracie, her eyes on Jacob. "Yes, let's do that."

7

Mom sent Gracie to her room to pack a bag with pajamas and a toothbrush. Walter sat on the edge of her bed. Gracie had almost forgotten he was waiting there. "What's going on?" he said when Gracie came in.

Gracie fought back the urge to shout something about his big mouth. "You promised you wouldn't say anything."

"I didn't think they'd tell your mom." Walter's eyes were red and puffy. "I don't understand what Gertrude Winters has to do with us. Why were they talking about going to get her?"

"Were you eavesdropping?" For some reason, this made Gracie like Walter a little better. He always seemed like such a goody two-shoes.

"Did you have something to do with her disappearing?"

As much as Gracie would have liked to have someone to talk to, someone who'd understand, she knew she'd only make Mom angrier if she told Walter the truth now. "You have to ask your parents. I need to pack."

Gracie closed the door behind Walter and whirled around her room. How could it be possible that she'd never see again the rose-colored bedspread, the fairy-tale posters taped to the walls, her favorite quotes from books that she had carefully selected and then hand-painted to the ceiling with glow-in-the-dark paint so she could read them in bed at night? Her favorite was from *A Little Princess*, and she liked to think about it as she fell asleep: "People who live in the story one is writing ought to come forward . . . tap the writing person on the shoulder and say, 'Hallo, what about me?'"

Now the quote seemed silly—wasn't that what she had tried to do with Gertrude Winters, say 'here I am'? And yet she had failed miserably. She shoved the book Gertrude Winters had signed into her backpack. No point hiding it from Mom now. On her dresser mirror, she'd taped a photo of herself and Mom from their trip to Disney World last year. They were laughing in front of the Cinderella castle, arms wrapped around one another, both wearing sparkly tiaras. Gracie pulled the picture free and slipped it into her pocket.

She ran into Mom in the hallway, who was dragging suitcases into her bedroom. "Let me stay with you," Gracie said. "I don't want to go."

Mom pulled Gracie into a hug. "I'm sorry," she said. "I'll be there in a few hours."

"I don't even know him!" For the smallest moment, with her face buried in Mom's shirt, the comforting scent of Mom's peppermint perfume enveloping her, she nearly had the nerve to ask Mom if Jacob was her father. But then Mom let her go and returned to the suitcases, and Gracie's courage flickered out.

"You know Walter, and he's going too." Mom spoke matter-of-factly, as if they were discussing something normal, like going to a birthday party. "You two will be safer with Jacob."

"What about you?" Gracie followed Mom into her bedroom.

"Don't worry about me. I'll be fast. Cassandra's not going to be able to find us that quickly." Mom set the suitcase on her bed and unzipped it.

"Then why do *I* have to go now?"

"Gracie, don't argue with me. Just trust me and do what I say." Mom creaked open the trunk at the foot of her bed.

Gracie watched as Mom packed the trunk's contents into the suitcase: photographs, cards, a necklace Gracie had strung for Mom's birthday when she was seven. She'd stayed up all night threading beads on a string. Memories of when they pretended their lives were normal—now everything was different. "I've always trusted you!" Gracie said. "And look what happened."

Mom paused in her packing, a Christmas ornament Gracie had made out of Popsicle sticks poised in her hand. "If you'd done what I said, we wouldn't even be in this mess. If you had obeyed me and not gone to see Gertrude Winters—"

"And if you'd told me what the parchment did, I never would have brought it to show her!" Tears came now, though Gracie couldn't tell if she was crying from fear, shame, or anger. "You're as much to blame as I am! If you hadn't kept secrets from me. . . . Why don't you trust me?"

Mom set the ornament on the bed and took Gracie's hand. "It's not that I don't trust you. And honestly, Gracie, I don't know much more than you do. I was afraid if you knew how to use the parchment, you might try to go back into the story."

"Why would I do that? You said I die in the story." Gracie wiped her nose on her sleeve.

Mom's face sagged. "But you were always so fascinated with it, wanting to know what happened in the story. I thought you might . . . I don't know." Mom squeezed Gracie's hand tighter. "Please go with Jacob. Trust me this one time. If you do, I'll tell you everything I know when I get there, all right? No more secrets."

There was something in Mom's expression that made her appear so small, so much like a deflated balloon, that Gracie could only nod and wrap her arms around Mom's waist. "No more secrets."

❧

Jacob drove an old pickup truck that smelled like moldy cheese. Gracie and Walter squeezed into the front seat beside him, Walter silent in the middle, Gracie pressed against the door. She jammed her backpack into the space by her feet. The floor was littered with what looked like gardening tools and one very large knife in a leather sheath. "I do a lot of hunting and gardening," Jacob said.

Walter sucked in his cheeks and wedged his backpack over Gracie's, kicking the knife out of the way. "What's going on?" he hissed in Gracie's ear. "My parents won't tell me anything."

Gracie shrugged, sneaking a glance at Jacob. He must have heard Walter, because he reached over as if to pat his shoulder and then let his hand flop awkwardly at his side. "I'm sure they'll explain everything when they get to my house."

Gracie turned to look at her house once more as Jacob's truck pulled from the curb. The lights were on, and she saw Mom's silhouette through the curtains in her bedroom window, leaning over the bed and packing. Gracie swallowed a lump in her throat. Surely this wouldn't be the last time Gracie saw her house. They'd come back once they were certain it was safe. Mom was being overly cautious, as usual.

Jacob hunched over the steering wheel, the headlights a dim glow on the rain-slick streets. They drove out of town, twisting onto country highways, finally turning onto a gravel road lined with pines as tall as houses, which loomed black against the night sky. They followed this for nearly half an hour until Jacob veered onto a path that wasn't a road at all. Branches scraped the truck as they squeezed through, headlights bouncing over the rough terrain. Finally they entered a small clearing and stopped beside a pop-up camper not much bigger than the truck. "Home sweet home," Jacob said.

"You live in a camper?" Walter turned to Jacob, his mouth wide.

"I like to be away from it all."

Gracie and Walter scurried after Jacob, wiping rain out of their eyes. The camper door was wedged shut, and Jacob jiggled it open and offered Gracie and Walter each a hand to totter inside; the front step was missing. Gracie's shoes skidded over the gritty floor as she climb-hopped in. Jacob flicked on a camping lantern, casting everything in a harsh, bluish glow.

On either end of the camper were beds. One was made up with blankets and pillows, the other piled in yellowed newspapers and books with titles like *Be Your Best Self* and *The Art of Now*. Beside the door was a built-in table with bench seats. On the opposite wall, covered in dirty dishes, peanut butter jars, water jugs, a gas burner, and loaves of bread, was a counter with a sink. A cooler rested beneath the table.

Jacob took Gracie and Walter's backpacks and set them on the bed. He wiped off the bench seats with a dishrag and gestured for them to sit down. "Do either of you want anything to eat?" he asked. "I'm not much of a cook, but—"

"I'm not hungry." Gracie leaned across the table to open the curtain. Soon she'd see headlights, and Mom would be here. She checked her phone. It was nearly midnight.

Walter slid onto the bench beside Gracie. "Someone needs to tell me what's going on."

"I know you're worried," Jacob said. "But your parents are smart people. They've evaded Queen Cassandra for years; it's not like she's going to get them now."

"I don't even know who this queen-person is," Walter said. "Or *you* for that matter."

"No one's told you about me?" Jacob's eyes rested on Gracie.

Gracie thought of all the times she'd heard her mother call Jacob's name in her sleep, but she didn't say this aloud. "No."

Jacob plucked at his beard.

Gracie gathered courage to ask her next question. This was not how she'd planned to find out about her father, and her chest felt tight, like once when she had fallen doing a cartwheel and had the wind knocked out of her. When she was younger she'd rehearsed this moment in her mind, the way she would meet her father for the first time, but now she couldn't recall any of the things she planned to say. She settled for, "How do you know our parents?"

Jacob poured water from one of the jugs into a chipped coffee mug. His hands were unsteady, and water slopped over the edge and onto the floor. He swore under his breath as he used a towel to mop it up. "I fled Bondoff with your parents," he said finally. "But I didn't want to stay in the city with them. Life seemed less risky here, a safer place to hide from Cassandra, and I couldn't get used to the noises and crowds in the outside world. Life is quieter in a story, in some ways."

Gracie watched him closely, wondering if he was telling the truth, if that's all there was to it. If he was her father, surely he wouldn't have left Gracie and Mom because he wanted to live in a camper in the woods. Maybe he really was just a friend of Mom's. "But why did—" she began.

"Why do you all keep talking about stories?" Walter asked. "And why do we have to hide because some author lady went missing? I saw Gracie come out of that bathroom. I'm sure she didn't have anything to do with it."

Jacob opened the camper door and peered into the night. "The rain's stopping," he said. "Your parents should be here before long. They'll explain everything then."

8

Gracie woke to sun streaming through the camper window, her cheek stuck to the tabletop. A fly buzzed, and she swatted it away. Walter snored beside her, his mouth open, glasses askew. She must have fallen asleep while she waited for Mom. Why hadn't Mom woken her when she came in? Gracie jolted upright, expecting to see Mom lying on the bed, but the camper was empty except for Jacob and Walter. Jacob slept on top of his blankets, still in blue jeans. Gracie peeked out the window, but Jacob's truck was the only vehicle in the yard. Gracie dug her phone out of her pocket and dialed Mom's cell, but it went straight to voicemail. Gracie shook Walter awake, and Jacob bolted from the bed, bumping his head on the ceiling.

"You told us they'd be here by now," Gracie said.

Jacob rubbed his forehead and went outside, and Gracie and Walter followed. The grass was wet from the rain the night before. Jacob stared at his truck. "It might've taken them some time to finish packing," Jacob said. "Or maybe they had trouble finding the place."

"My mom's not answering her phone," Gracie said.

"I wouldn't worry too much about that," Jacob said. "There's lousy reception out here. Or her battery could be dead. That's probably why they didn't call."

"My dad's not answering either," Walter said, his phone pressed to his ear.

Jacob stuffed his fists into his pants pockets and stared at the treeline. "Come on, I'll fix you both some breakfast. They'll be here soon."

෴

There wasn't electricity in the camper, and when Gracie turned the knob on the sink, no water came out.

"It's not hooked up." Jacob passed her the water jug. "I get water from town or the rain barrel. I suppose you're not used to that like I am. It's the way things are in Bondoff."

Walter wrinkled his nose. "Bondoff? Where's that?"

Jacob chewed his lip and slathered peanut butter onto bread. Something familiar hovered about him, a feeling Gracie had met him before. Jacob handed her one of the sandwiches, and his eyes met hers. Embarrassed that he'd caught her staring, Gracie looked away and busied herself peeling the crusts off the bread.

"Maybe we should go look for our parents," Walter said.

"They'll be here." Jacob filled a kettle with water and set it atop a propane burner. "I'm sure they've got a good reason for whatever's keeping them. Do you two want hot chocolate?"

Gracie tried to read Jacob's expression, wondering whether he was really unconcerned or simply trying to soothe Walter, but he kept his back to her as he fiddled with the knob on the burner. Peanut butter stuck in Gracie's throat.

Walter sat across from Gracie at the table; his eyes were red, his words toppling over one another. "I know you're mad at me for telling you were at the bookstore, and I'm sorry if I got you in trouble, but I'm worried about my parents too. What's going on?"

Gracie brushed crumbs off her lap. Walter was right. She didn't like it when Mom kept secrets from her, and now she was doing the same thing to Walter. He must be frightened to be sent off in the middle of the night with no explanation. "I'm not mad at you," she said.

Jacob must've been having similar thoughts because he finally turned to look at them, leaning against the sink, his hands clasped at his waist. "Have your parents told you anything about Gertrude Winters?"

Walter shook his head.

"She wrote a book about us," Jacob said.

"Why would she do that?"

"Because she made us up." Gracie had been wanting to tell Walter this for so long, now that the moment had come, the words poured out in a gush. "She created us. We'd still be in the story, except our parents took us out of the story and into the outside world so we could hide from Queen Cassandra. Cassandra's the villain in the story."

Gracie glanced at Jacob. He smiled weakly, but Walter rested his head in his palms. "That's very funny, Gracie."

"I'm not joking," Gracie said. "That's why I wanted to talk to Gertrude Winters—I wanted to find out what happened in the story she wrote about us—but everything went wrong."

Walter snorted. "Yup, we're storybook characters, and a villain is after us."

"It's true!" Flames crackled faintly, firelight flashing under a pale moon. For so long, Gracie had wished to be able to talk to Walter about the glimmers, and now he didn't believe her. Gracie *knew* it was true: she saw it in her dreams all the time. "You see her," Gracie said suddenly.

"What?"

"Do you still dream about the lady?"

"How do you know about the lady?"

"You told me when we were little that you saw her, Walter." She leaned toward him over the table, her elbows resting on either side of her plate. "I dream about her too. It's what I was talking about the other day, remember? About visions that seem like memories? The lady is Queen Cassandra. The dreams are about things that were supposed to happen in the story but didn't. My mom told me."

"You both see her?" The spoon Jacob was holding slipped from his fingers and clattered to the floor. "What else do you see?"

"Fire," Gracie said. "That's mostly it."

"Having dreams about someone doesn't prove that we're storybook characters." Walter shoved his plate aside, his sandwich untouched. "I'm sure there's a logical explanation."

"If it's not true, then why were our parents running, huh?"

Walter pinched the bridge of his nose between his fingers. "I don't know. Maybe they're all suffering under some kind of delusion. Or maybe they had some kind of criminal involvement."

"My mom's not a criminal!"

"That's not the point. The point is there could be all kinds of reasons for what's going on that don't resort to explanations that are impossible. The scientific method relies on testing and observation."

"Maybe science can explain Bondoff," Gracie said. "Maybe it's in another galaxy or something."

Walter turned to Jacob. "You don't believe this, do you?"

"So you're a man of science?" Jacob said.

Walter nodded. "Indeed."

"Isn't that intriguing, that even out of the story, you still grew up to be a scientist?"

Walter scowled.

"You've read the story?" Gracie said. "What did it say about me?"

Jacob collected the sandwich plates and wiped them clean with a paper towel. Sweat gathered in little beads at his hairline. "Well, I haven't read the whole story," he said. "I just remember hearing that part about Walter. Your father's the only one who's read the whole story, so, of course, I don't really know much about what it says."

"You know my father? Where is he?" The words flew out of her mouth before she could stop them, before she'd had time to register that Jacob had referred to her father as someone else. Not him.

Jacob used a potholder to remove the kettle from the burner. The mugs rattled as he set them on the table, and Jacob shoved his trembling hands into his pants pockets. "Your mother didn't tell you about him?"

"Only a little." The words came out in a croak.

"Well, he's not really as bad as all that."

"Bad?"

"Maybe we should wait until your mom gets here."

"Please." Gracie's eyes met Jacob's, and he looked away quickly and stared at the table. "I've wondered about him my whole life. My mom won't talk about him."

Jacob was silent for a long while, and when he finally spoke again, his voice was low and hoarse. "What you've got to understand is the kind of world we come from. It's a place of fear. Queen Cassandra knows everything there; she rules everything. She's not the kind of person you say no to. When she set her eyes on your father, it wouldn't have been easy to say no."

"What do you mean 'set her eyes on him'?"

Jacob poured the steaming water, and some sloshed over the edge of the cup and onto the table. "I thought your mother would've told you that part." Jacob mopped up the spill and stirred in cocoa powder from a paper packet. "Your father thought he was in love," he said finally, sliding the cocoa across the table to Gracie. "With Cassandra. He left your mother when you were a baby."

"My father was in love with that woman?" The heat from the mug burned Gracie's fingers, but she barely felt it. She thought of the woman of the story glimmers, her cruel beauty, Mom's sweet softness.

Jacob flushed pink. "He didn't know anything about the story then, Gracie! As soon as Cassandra showed him the Vademecum and he read what it said about you, he stole two of its pages and got you out of the story. He did the right thing in the end!"

Jacob was speaking too loudly, spit gathering in the corners of his mouth. Gracie stared into her cocoa. Powder clumped in gritty balls on the rim. All this time, she'd dreamed of what her father was like, made excuses for why he wasn't in her life, and in the end, it was something both terrible and ordinary; he would rather be with this Cassandra woman than Gracie and Mom. She wished Walter wouldn't stare at her like that, his head tilted sympathetically, as if he was expecting her to burst into tears. Gracie wasn't sad, just angry.

"Go with me," Walter said.

Gracie turned to him. "What?"

"They had Latin at science camp last summer. *Vade mecum* is Latin for 'go with me.'"

"Why do you always need to show off how smart you are?" She regretted the words instantly; it wasn't Walter's fault that her father had left her, and now he had that hurt-puppy look on his face.

"I'm not! Jacob said something about *vade mecum*. I was only translating."

Jacob rested his hand on Walter's shoulder. "It's also the name for a kind of book, one kept with you always. That's the Vademecum Cassandra has."

Gracie gripped her mug, letting the steam bathe her face, wanting to apologize for her outburst but feeling too ashamed. "You said my father read it," she said finally.

Jacob knelt beside the bed and pulled a small wooden box from the cupboard beneath it. "The Vademecum is the book the parchment pages come from." He removed a piece of parchment identical to the one Mom owned, before Gracie lost it. "Its pages act as a kind of portal: they allow Cassandra to travel between the story world and the outside world, but it's more than that." Jacob paused thoughtfully. "Before we left, Cassandra had no desire to travel to the outside world because she had more power in Bondoff than she does here. The Vademecum is like a kind of story bible, a guidebook; the entire story Gertrude Winters created about us is written inside. Cassandra keeps it with her always. She can read about everything in the story world, past, present, and future. Do you know how much power that gives a person, always knowing what will happen before it actually happens? The people in Bondoff think she's like a god. When your father saw what was written in the Vademecum, he tore two pages from it"—Jacob gestured to the parchment in his hand—"and used their power to take us out of the story." Jacob sank onto the bench beside Gracie. "Cassandra can't read about things in the real world the way she can read about things happening in Bondoff. It's why she hasn't been able to find us here; she doesn't know exactly where we live."

Gracie's stomach felt sick. "Until I talked to Gertrude Winters."

Jacob's face was grim. "Yes."

"This is ridiculous," Walter said.

"Let him touch it," Gracie said.

Jacob handed the parchment to Walter. Gracie knew Walter must be experiencing the tingly sensation she always felt when she touched it, the magic that radiated from it, the desire to close her eyes and sink into it. He held his mouth in a lopsided way, as if he wanted to throw up.

"What did the story say?" Walter asked.

"It said we would die," Gracie whispered.

Jacob looked at her sharply.

"People don't die because a book says so," Walter said.

"I remember it," Gracie said.

"You remember dying?" Jacob said.

"Not exactly." Gracie traced her finger along a line of crumbs on the table. How to explain the fear, the choking smoke, the blistering heat? "Mom calls the visions glimmers. I see a fire; I dream about it. That's why Mom told me about Bondoff in the first place, because I was so scared of the story glimmers and she needed to explain them to me."

Jacob stared at Gracie a moment before continuing. He spoke slowly, as if measuring his words carefully. "Gertrude Winters wrote you would die at the end of the story, but your father wouldn't let that happen. He saved you."

"What did the story say about me?" Walter asked.

Jacob ran his fingers through his hair, leaving a lock sticking upright and giving him a wild look. "Gracie's father read that you and I would die in the story too. He helped us out too."

"So my father is here?" Gracie said.

Jacob wiped the back of his hand across his mouth. "No. Your mother couldn't forgive him, so he stayed back in Bondoff."

Jacob was looking at her as if he pitied her, but Gracie didn't feel the way Jacob seemed to expect her to. "I never knew my father," Gracie said. "I couldn't care less what he does. He shouldn't have done that to my mom."

Jacob's cheek twitched. "He *is* the one who got us out of the book and saved our lives. He's not all bad."

"Yeah, well, I guess he did one thing right. That still doesn't make him father of the year." She spat the words. Hours ago, she had thought she was meeting her father for the first time, and instead, this man was telling her these awful things. No wonder Mom didn't like to talk about her dad. He'd left Mom for a woman who wanted Gracie dead. Still, something bothered her about Jacob's story. If Jacob was simply someone who'd left the story with them, why should Mom have called out to him in her sleep?

"I want to go home," Walter said.

9

Walter spent the rest of the morning reading in the sun, not talking to either Gracie or Jacob. He spread a blanket on the grass and sat on it with his backpack. It had apparently contained a stack of science books, because he surrounded himself with a circle of them, lining the blanket as if the books could protect him from everything that had happened. Gracie sat at the table and watched him through the window, alert for any sounds of a car. Jacob asked her about school and Mom as he attempted to tidy the filthy camper. His tone was casual, but Gracie noted he glanced out the window as often as she did.

Around noon Jacob produced a deck of cards. "Are you up for a game?" he said.

Gracie shrugged. The last time she'd played cards was with Mom.

"Do you know how to play Queen's Heart?"

Something like fear and homesickness stirred in Gracie's stomach. It was a simple game, similar to what kids at school called Old Maid. Mom said in Bondoff they called it Queen's Heart. "Mom taught me."

As he shuffled cards, Jacob said, "You look like your mother." His cheeks were pink, and he spoke quietly, as if he had suddenly grown shy.

"Do you think so?" People said this, sometimes, but Gracie thought they were only being kind. Mom was short and petite, with freckles that danced across her nose and a smile that made you want to smile back. Gracie was taller than her now by two inches, her curly hair was always messy, and her mouth was as often scowling as smiling. She didn't mean to frown, but she had a tendency to screw up her lips when she was thinking intently about something.

"I first met her when she was your age," Jacob said as he dealt. "You look like she did then."

"You knew my mom when she was a girl?" Gracie picked up her cards.

"Bondoff's not very big. Everyone knows everyone there."

"You knew my father too?"

Jacob frowned at his cards. "Do you think maybe it wasn't his fault what he did? Gertrude Winters is the one who wrote the story about him. Maybe your dad couldn't help but be the person she wrote about."

"Mom says it doesn't matter what Gertrude Winters wrote about us, that we can be whoever we want." Gracie lay down a pair of fives.

"What do *you* say?"

"I don't know. I think it would be easier to figure out who I am if I could read the story Gertrude Winters wrote." Gracie drew from Jacob's hand and laid down another pair. "Tell me the things you remember about my parents."

Jacob's mouth twitched into a smile. "Your mother was a daredevil," he said. "She was always getting into trouble."

"Mom? No, she's scared of everything."

"She's just cautious. She doesn't want to risk Cassandra finding you. You should have seen her when she was younger." Jacob laughed.

"What?"

"I was remembering one time when Elizabeth was your age. One of the queen's guards lived down the road from her. Most of the guards live in the castle, but a few have houses out in the town, so they can spy on people better, I suppose. This one was a nasty guy, and he had a little yappy dog that he liked to kick around. Elizabeth hated that guard; she always had a soft spot for dogs. Anyway, she slept in the attic, and she used to climb out her bedroom window and cross over the rooftops until she was on this guy's roof. There was a crack in the roof, and she could see him sleeping below. She used to talk to him through the crack, tell him to give up the dog, made him think he was hearing ghosts. He finally gave up the dog to make the voices stop, and Elizabeth took it in."

"Whatever happened to the dog?"

"It was old. It didn't live long after that. But at least its last years were happy with Elizabeth. She was crushed when it died." Jacob laid down two sevens.

"I can't imagine Mom doing something as dangerous as climbing on roofs."

"Can't you? I think your mom is the type of person who'd do anything to protect someone she cares about."

Gracie thought how brave Mom must have been to take her out of the home she knew, the story-world of Bondoff, and into this world. "I miss her." Gracie set her cards aside. "I'm worried that she's not here. Do you think we should go back and look for her?"

"Gracie, I promised your mother I would keep you safe. That's a promise I intend to keep. She wouldn't want me to take you home, not if I thought it was dangerous. She wants me to protect you, first and foremost."

"So you *do* think they're in danger?" Gracie hadn't noticed Walter appear in the doorway, but now he settled on the bench beside her. He'd pinned one of his backpack buttons to his shirt. It read: "Be a science girl or guy: always ask what and why."

Jacob set his cards aside as well. "Look, I didn't say anything happened to them. I only meant you're safer here. They told us to wait here for them."

"Do you think we should call the police?" Walter's voice was strained.

"It wouldn't do any good." Jacob gathered the cards and slid them back into their pouch. "If Cassandra did find them, she would use the Vademecum to take them back into the story world. The police can't help them there."

"Will you both stop with this story nonsense!" Walter's face was pink.

Gracie ignored him. "But you still have a piece of the parchment. If Cassandra did get them, we could go into the story to rescue them, right? That's what you said at my house, that you could go in to rescue Winters."

"That was a hypothetical," Jacob said. "And that was before I had the responsibility of keeping you two safe. Besides, you don't know that Cassandra got them. Let's give them a little longer. We'll deal with 'what ifs' when the time comes. Chances are your parents feel terrible that they've got us all worried over something simple like a flat tire or a blown gasket."

೧೪

But as dinnertime approached, Mom still hadn't come, and Gracie's temper was on edge. She could do nothing but stare out the window and wait. Walter sat beside her. He was silent, but even the sound of his breathing annoyed her. Jacob heated cans of chili in a saucepan over the camp stove. Walter crumbled saltine crackers into his.

Gracie felt hot all over, and a story glimmer seemed to lurk on the edge of her consciousness. The scent of smoke hung in the air, and it irritated her that no one else seemed to smell it. "I don't know how either of you can eat at a time like this."

"There's no point in starving ourselves," Jacob said.

"Why aren't you more worried?" Sweat crept along the back of Gracie's neck. "Don't you care about my mom at all?"

Jacob stared into his chili. "The important thing is to keep you safe," he said quietly.

Gracie shoved her bowl away. "If it was *your* family in danger, you wouldn't sit here."

"It is my family in danger!" Jacob's cheeks flushed, and he slammed his palm onto the table. Walter made a little squeaking sound, and Jacob's face drained of color. He closed his eyes and spoke slowly. "I only meant, I don't have family of my own. And I don't know anyone here in the outside world. You all are the closest thing to family I have."

Gracie's head ached with the effort of keeping the glimmers at bay. She pulled her damp hair off her neck. "If you really cared about our parents, you'd help find them."

Jacob picked a bean out with his spoon, then let it fall back into the bowl. "I'll take a drive. I'll check the house and see if they're still there."

Gracie sprang from the table, the dishes clattering. "We're coming with you."

"No."

"You're going to leave us here alone?" Walter said. "Because you're scared of some made-up lady? Wouldn't leaving us here be more dangerous than bringing us? There could be bears. Or creepy strangers. Or—"

"Fine," Jacob said. "But both of you are staying in the truck."

10

The drive seemed to take forever. They sat squashed into the front seat of the truck again, and though none of them said it, they all seemed to fear the worst. Gracie had watched Jacob slide the parchment page and a pocketknife into his jeans pocket when he thought they weren't looking, and she and Walter both stashed their backpacks onto the floor of the truck. Gracie leaned forward as they drove, peering out the window, alert for any sign of Mom or Walter's parents. She thought of the argument she and Mom had the last time she saw her. Now she wondered if all this time, Mom had been right to be so fearful. If Gracie had stayed away from Winters, none of this would have happened.

Darkness fell by the time they reached town. They stopped at Walter's house first because it was closer. Walter gave Jacob his spare key, and Jacob went inside, but he came back out shortly afterward, shaking his head. "No sign of them," he said, hopping back into the driver's seat. "And there's no car in the garage."

Gracie knew something was wrong as soon as they reached her house. Both Mom's car and Walter's parents' car were in the driveway, but the house was dark. Jacob parked down the block under a streetlight and turned the truck off. "Stay here," Jacob said. "I mean it."

"But Jacob—"

Jacob's face was harsh in the gloom. "Under no circumstances are you to leave this truck." He pulled the parchment out of his pocket and handed it to Walter. "Keep this with you. If Cassandra is in there, I don't want her to get it. I'll be right back."

Walter nodded. His face was stricken as he stared at his parents' car.

"If Cassandra might be there, shouldn't we come with to help you?" Gracie said.

"Absolutely not. I'm just going to check things out. I don't want to have to worry about keeping you out of trouble too. Lock the doors and don't open them until I get back."

"But—"

But Jacob had already closed the door and was gone, creeping through the shadows toward Gracie's house. Why were the cars still there? Was her mother in trouble? She watched as Jacob disappeared inside the house. The windows were dark, the silence not even broken by crickets chirping. In the distance, a dog howled, long and low. Gracie put her hand on the door latch, and Walter yanked it away.

"What are you doing?"

"Don't you want to find out what happened to our parents? What if Cassandra is in there and they need us?"

"Jacob told us to stay here."

"You're going to do everything Jacob says now?"

Walter thrust his phone in Gracie's face. "No, I'm going to give him five minutes, and then I'm going to call the police. I don't believe in this Cassandra person, but I do believe in robbers. What if our parents were kidnapped? What if it's the Mafia? I told you they could be involved in something criminal." Walter rubbed his temples. "I feel like I'm going to be sick."

Gracie pressed her face to the window. All was still. Jacob hadn't even turned any lights on in the house.

"Stay here then. I'm going to check things out."

She slid from the car before Walter could stop her.

࿇

The front door hung ajar, and Gracie eased it wider so she could slip inside. She stood in the doorway a moment, letting her eyes adjust to the gloom. Books were strewn everywhere, their pages torn out, one of the bookshelves tipped on its side. Furniture was upended, clothes and knick-knacks scattered across the floor. Something was different about the air, too: it didn't have the usual smell she associated with home, but rather something stale and empty. Jacob stood on the far side of the living room with his back to Gracie, staring at pictures on the wall. A photo of Gracie and Mom hung askew, and Jacob straightened it. Gracie stepped over the piles of books and made her way toward him, her heart thumping jerkily. "Mom?" Her voice sounded like a hiccup.

Jacob turned, panic etched across his face. "I told you to wait in the car."

"Where's my mom?"

In seconds, Jacob had crossed the room and grabbed her by the wrist. "We need to get out of here."

"Did Cassandra take her?"

Jacob's voice was hoarse. "I think so."

"We'll go save her then, right?" Gracie could feel hysteria growing inside her, like a spark catching tinder, and the words were louder than she intended.

"You don't understand; we can't go back to Bondoff. It's not like here. When you're in the story, what's written about you controls things. You don't know what would happen."

Jacob was dragging Gracie toward the door, and she wrenched her hand away and headed toward Mom's bedroom. "I'm not going anywhere except to find my mom."

"It's not that easy." Jacob sped after her. "Everything's different there. You already act quite a bit like your character, and the story can make us do things. It can make us—I know, okay? I did things in the story, bad things, things my family will never forgive me for." Jacob's voice cracked. "I'd like to think I wouldn't have done them if Winters hadn't written them about me."

"Surely you don't mean that." The voice was like sandpaper, as if the speaker had something caught in her throat. Gracie's stomach lurched, and she jerked her head toward the sound coming from Mom's room. The hall light flickered on, and a woman stepped into its glow. Jacob lunged forward, thrusting Gracie behind him, so he stood between her and the woman.

She was the woman Gracie dreamed of, though more vivid now that she was standing only feet away. She smelled of sage and incense, and her hair—black with a few wisps of gray mixed in—was pulled severely into a bun. She was startlingly beautiful, with high, sharp cheekbones, full red lips, creamy skin, and black eyebrows that slanted in a way that made her look amused. She wore a black dress that flapped about her ankles and a string of gold pencils tied like keys at her waist. A crown glinted on her head, and her hands were heavy with jeweled rings. She held a brown leather book, too, and something about the book forced Gracie's eyes to it as if she couldn't look away. The woman opened it to the middle, and something shimmery seemed to emanate from its blank pages; it reminded Gracie of pictures of the Milky Way.

"Jacob, you started off very well, but perhaps you are not a storyteller, my dear." The words were pronounced slowly, almost tenderly, caressing the syllables, and Gracie looked to Jacob, but he seemed frozen in place, his body stiffened. "Have you grown sentimental in your old age? You've been away from me for too long."

"Leave her alone," Jacob said.

"I can't, of course. I'm only doing what's right. You belong in the story."

Jacob shoved Gracie. "Run," he said, but Gracie's limbs felt heavy, as if something had hooked her behind her belly button and was pulling her slowly like a tether, drawing her toward the book. It was smaller than Gracie had expected, less than an inch thick, no longer than Gracie's hand, its binding worn. What secrets did it contain?

"Where's my mom?" Gracie said.

"Come with me," Cassandra said. "I can take you to her. Don't be afraid."

Cassandra stepped toward them, the book outstretched in front of her, and Gracie inched slowly back. This was the book Jacob had told her about, the Vademecum the parchment pages came from, the book that contained a copy of Gertrude Winters's story. Here, an arms-length away, were all the answers to Gracie's questions, but Mom's warnings tugged at her memory. "No," Gracie said. "You want to kill me."

"Kill you?" Cassandra's lips drew back into a grimace, her teeth flashing, and she turned to Jacob. "What kind of lies have you been telling her?"

Jacob shook his head. "I didn't—Elizabeth—"

Before he could finish his sentence, Cassandra had pressed the book to his chest, and he dropped to his knees, his arms flung out to his sides, as if about to embrace someone. His skin began to shimmer and fade, as if he was dissolving into the book. His mouth moved soundlessly.

"Your father lies," Cassandra said.

Gracie's eyes flicked from Jacob to Cassandra. "Jacob's my father?"

"You don't know anything, do you?" Cassandra wagged her head sadly, clicking her tongue against her teeth. "It isn't fair, is it? The way they kept you from your destiny. Put your hand on the book. Come with me, dear, and I'll tell you your entire story."

"And take me to Mom?"

Cassandra winced, as if something pained her, but she nodded slowly. "If you must."

Gracie edged closer to Cassandra, to the book. What would Mom want her to do? She'd always warned her to stay away from Cassandra, but now Mom needed her. And Cassandra had promised to tell her everything; she didn't seem as bad as Mom always said. Mom hadn't told her the truth about the parchment or her father. Why should Gracie obey her now? Gracie held out her hand.

"Gracie?"

She turned. Walter stood behind her, holding the parchment. It shimmered and pulsed, like Cassandra's book, and as soon as Gracie saw it, the fog in her mind cleared. Mom would not want her to go with Cassandra. Mom would want her to flee. Jacob had told her to flee.

"Run!" Gracie shouted. She clutched at Walter's hand, and the two of them sped down the hall, away from Cassandra, from the book, from Jacob. Gracie glanced over her shoulder as she fled, just in time to see Jacob disappear completely, and then she and Walter banged through the door and out of the house, Cassandra's footsteps hammering behind them.

11

They ran. Gracie's heart pounded and her feet skidded across the grass as they cut across backyards, darting through shadows, always feeling as if in a moment someone would catch her by the hair. She would fall to her knees and be taken, just like Mom, like Walter's parents, like Jacob. They wove past decks and swing sets and barbecues, clothes flapping on a line, signs of ordinary life that seemed foreign to her now. She had always felt different, but she hadn't realized *how* different until she had spoken to Cassandra and felt the enormity of what she was truly facing. For years she had known Cassandra was after her, and she had seen the glimmers, but she realized as she sprinted over a garden hose that she hadn't truly believed it until now. She'd thought if she could only find Mom again, things would be all right. But now? There was no returning to the way things had been before. Home was no longer the haven she'd thought it was; safety was an illusion. Mom had been right all along.

She had no destination in mind, but when they reached the end of the street the elementary school was on, both made for the building without speaking. The doors were locked, but Gracie glanced over her shoulder and, not seeing Cassandra, pulled Walter around the corner of the building toward the playground—a jumble of jungle gyms and monkey bars and swings. She and Walter ducked inside a tunnel slide where they'd be hidden, and Gracie pressed her legs against the plastic-tube walls to keep herself from sliding down. Walter did the same, sitting so close their foreheads touched. Gracie could feel the heat of Walter's breath on her.

"You believe me now?" Gracie hissed, but she wasn't really mad, and Walter opened and closed his mouth, as if gulping back words or trying to suck in oxygen, a little like a fish.

"She got Jacob," Walter said, and Gracie nodded.

"Is he dead?"

"I don't think so—I think he's in the story."

"What do we do now?"

"Cassandra has our parents." Gracie eyed the parchment still clutched in Walter's fist. "She told me so."

"We should call the police."

"It won't do any good; they won't believe us."

"Do you have a better idea?"

Gracie pried the parchment from Walter's fingers and smoothed it out against the wall of the slide. "When Gertrude Winters wrote her name on my mom's parchment, she disappeared. Jacob said it meant she had gone into the story. We should be able to get in the same way."

"I thought you said we died in the story?"

"And I thought you said people don't die because a story says so?" Gracie sighed. "Look, we won't go in long enough to die. We'll go in, get our parents, and get out. Cassandra won't even know we're there." Even as she said the words, Gracie could feel fear rising. What was it Jacob said? He'd said it wasn't as simple as just going into the story world, that the story could make you do things you didn't want to do. But what did that mean?

"Gracie, I don't know."

"We have to at least try! We can't leave them."

Walter was silent.

"We need something to write with," Gracie said.

Walter twisted around and unzipped his backpack. He handed Gracie a pen. Gracie took a deep breath. The parchment hummed beneath her fingers. The pen trembled in her hand. Walter placed his fingers over hers. "We'll write our names together," he said.

Walter's hand was comforting, even if his palm was sweaty. The pen glided over the parchment as they signed it, and Gracie could read the letters even in the dark, for they shone as if lit from behind. Before she'd had time to wonder about this, the parchment grew heavier, as if she had a great weight in her hands. The parchment faded and disappeared, but its heft remained, pulling her hands down, down, and the heaviness settling upon her grew stronger still, gathering strength until she felt as if she were falling, or sinking, as if she were underwater. Her ears popped as if the air pressure had changed, and all she could hear was a rustling like turning pages. And then she was being squeezed, her vision blurred—she could see nothing, though she could hear whispering all around, the murmur of a million words blurred together; not all were distinguishable from the rest.

"Walter," she tried to scream as his fingers slipped from hers, but the whisper-words drowned out the sound of her own voice. "Once upon a time." "It was a dark and stormy night." "In a land called Bondoff, in a castle on a hill." Before she could make sense of any of it, the words were replaced by a roaring in her ears and she felt like she would throw up, until she knew nothing at all and everything was black.

༄༅

Sun filtered through the pines, and birds chirped in the distance. Gracie was lying on the ground, pine needles pressed into her face. Her whole body ached. She pushed herself into a sitting position. Behind her, something moved, and she whirled around. Walter lay on the ground too, just starting to wake, his backpack at his side. He rubbed his eyes and looked at Gracie. "Where are we?"

Gracie stood and brushed dirt from her jeans. "I don't know." She spotted something white at her feet and retrieved the parchment from the ground. It no longer glowed, but it was still warm, and she resisted the pull it seemed to have on her, the urge to close her eyes and hold it. She shoved it into her pocket. It was important she hang on to it. It would be the only way back home once she found Mom.

Gracie turned in a slow circle. Tall pines stretched endlessly on all sides. There wasn't another living thing in sight, other than the birds she could hear but not see. No path, no road, no sound of cars in the distance. For a moment, she felt unsteady, as if the world were rocking beneath her, much like being on a boat. Light seemed to shimmer on the edges of her vision, and she felt as if she turned her head suddenly she would see something lurking around the edges of things. But nothing happened, and the feeling passed. There was something strange about the air; it was clean and fresh, but not like a forest. It didn't smell like the pines all around her—what was it exactly? Yes, it smelled like paper, like when Gracie had stuck her nose between the pages of a book. But wasn't paper made out of trees? So perhaps this was the smell of trees. Either way, the sensation passed, and the paper smell was replaced with pine and dirt and leaves and all the odors Gracie would expect from a forest. Gracie had imagined Bondoff to be a terrible place, but this forest was rather pretty. But there was no trace of Mom. No sign of Jacob. No sign of anyone.

"We should get moving," Walter said. "We need to find our parents before that woman finds us."

Gracie nodded slowly. A funny feeling had swept over her; her hands and feet tingled, and something tapped the back of her brain, a sense she'd been here before. She pointed behind Walter, where the trees seemed to grow thinner. "I think that's the way to town."

Walter glanced where Gracie was pointing, then shook his head and squatted beside his backpack, examining his buttons. "That's how people get lost. One of my pins is a compass. We should stay headed north so we don't end up walking in circles."

Walter stared at the compass and then pointed in the direction opposite from the one Gracie had suggested. "That way."

Gracie looked over Walter's shoulder. There was no path no matter what way they headed, and at least with a compass, they'd have a direction. "All right," she said.

They'd only walked a few minutes, though, when the air grew heavy, as if they were traipsing through sludge, and yet there was nothing there. It was as if something was pushing them back, as if the air were water that they must wade through, until it grew even thicker and more solid and they could move no more. It was like an invisible wall stood before them. Gracie placed her hands in front of her, palms flat, resting them against the transparent wall. She could see trees ahead of her, on the other side, but she couldn't move toward them.

"It's like some kind of force field," Walter said.

Again, the funny feeling prickled, something familiar about the wall. It was disturbing, being trapped, as if the story was a prison they couldn't move outside of. "I think it's a barrier," Gracie said. "We must've come into the story right on the edge of it."

"Cool." Walter prodded the wall with his finger. "Can you imagine if the government got wind of this? If we could create an invisible barrier? I wish I had my science equipment. I'd love to study this."

Gracie shook her head. She couldn't feel excited like Walter. "We can't go outside the story's setting." Gracie trailed her hand along the wall, which left her fingertips tingling. "Doesn't it scare you at all?"

Walter looked up. "Why should it?"

"It feels like being locked in a cage."

Walter shrugged. "The barrier can't go on forever. We'll walk the other way."

And though Gracie was certain he was wrong, that this was not nearly so simple, she followed him anyway. Perhaps Mom had been right to be angry with Gertrude Winters for writing their story the way she had, tossing their lives around carelessly, as if they mattered no more than the flash of a pen, the click of a keystroke. Gracie and Walter plodded on, but Gracie couldn't help feeling like a prisoner, trapped in a story where she knew none of the rules.

12

They hiked for hours before the trees thinned, then cleared, and the forest opened onto a town that looked as if it had sprung from between the pages of a storybook.

A dirt road led to clusters of low buildings and shacks set along dusty winding streets, where pigs ran free and chickens pecked the dirt. In the distance, a castle loomed over everything, banners flapping from its stone towers. Gracie watched the castle uneasily, staying in the safety of the trees and clutching Walter's hand.

The streets were full of people calling out to one another, going about their business. Women peered from doorways in long ragged dresses, with babies (most of them naked) on their hips. The air smelled like manure and grilled meat. Gracie was reminded of a Renaissance fair she'd attended with her mother as she watched a crowd gathered around a low stone well. Her throat was parched.

"We need water," Walter said. "Do you suppose it'd be safe?"

"Look at us." Gracie gestured to her jeans, spotted now with dirt. She brushed a pine needle from her leg. "We'll stick out dressed like this, and we don't know what the story says. What if one of those people works for Cassandra?"

"How are we supposed to find our parents if we can't let anyone see us?"

"I don't know." The sight of the town had increased the tingly feeling, and Gracie sat on the ground and pulled her knees to her chest, her eyes scrunched tight. She touched the parchment in her pocket. In her mind she could see a small building, painted red. A wooden sign swung beside the door, and she saw a flash of herself mounting the steps, the scent of her mother's perfume wafting in the air.

"You look weirder than I do," Walter said.

Gracie's eyes snapped open. "What's that supposed to mean?"

Walter's cheeks grew red. "Not weird. I just meant because you're a girl."

"What's wrong with girls?"

"Nothing! But all the girls in the town are wearing dresses. You'll stand out more in pants than I will. Maybe you should stay here, and I can find clothes for us."

"You're not going off alone without me!"

"I won't go far. I bet I can buy something." Walter scrounged in his pocket and pulled out some folded bills. "My dad gave me my allowance the other day. I have ten dollars."

"Do you really expect these people to use our kind of money?"

Walter shrugged. "They might."

"They don't. And you'll only draw attention to yourself if you try to buy something."

"What am I supposed to do, steal?"

Gracie pressed her finger to her lip. "You could."

Walter edged away from her. "You think they go easy on criminals here? Haven't you ever read a fairy tale? They all have dungeons."

Gracie sighed. "We'll have to wait until it's dark to look for our parents. It's our best chance to go into town without being seen."

So they sat in the shade of the trees, watching the town. Gracie's mouth was so dry, it felt as if it had been stuffed with cotton balls. She licked her lips, watching the women who hauled buckets of water from the well and hoping one would be Mom, but none were. The longer she sat, the stronger the images of the red building became, until she was certain that was where she would find Mom. When the sun began to sink over the horizon and people started going into their homes, the streets emptying, Gracie stood and brushed dirt from her pants. "I think I know where we need to go."

ᘓᘏ

They circled the town, staying on the edge of the forest and trying to find a deserted section where they could enter without running into any people, although only a few seemed to wander at night. The moon was almost full, allowing them enough light to navigate, but this also meant they could more easily be spotted as well. Bondoff definitely was nothing like the world in which

Gracie had grown up. All of the buildings were small and low-slung, with sagging roofs and weedy lawns. Animal dung and food scraps littered the ground. Outside one of the houses was a bucket with a dipper in it, and they snuck into the yard and each drank from it before slipping into the woods again. Some of the homes had strange black claw-like things hanging over their doors, and it wasn't until they had passed several of them that Gracie recognized them as chicken feet. Other people had painted yellow eyes on the sides of the buildings, with crosses drawn through them. Gracie had read books where people used talismans for things. She wondered if these were to ward off magic, like warding off the evil eye. She normally didn't believe in things like that, but she wondered if in this story it worked. She wished she had a talisman right now. A dog barked in the distance.

"Gracie, look." Walter placed a hand on her arm.

Gracie turned. Walter pointed to a backyard, where someone had left blankets drying on a line. Before she could stop him, Walter had slipped out of the trees and into the yard. He tugged the blankets from the line, looked over his shoulder, and ducked back into the shadows. Gracie's heart beat so fast it felt as if all the air had left her body. "What are you doing?" she hissed. "Do you want everyone after us?"

"Put this on." Walter wrapped one of the blankets around her shoulders. It was thin and scratchy and smelled like a barn. "People here wear cloaks. If we have these on, we won't stand out so much." Walter fumbled with his backpack, unfastening one of his science buttons and using the pin on the back to secure the blanket at Gracie's throat. He did the same with the blanket he draped around his own shoulders. "There. Now we just need to figure out where to go."

Gracie brushed dirt from the blanket and tried not to think about the smell. "We're looking for a red house."

"I don't understand how you could suddenly know where your house is." The hollows beneath Walter's eyes were dark in the moonlight. "You haven't been there since you were a baby."

"How do you know people here wear cloaks? We didn't see anyone in one."

Walter was silent for a moment. "I don't know. I guess I just assumed. I mean, they probably do—"

Gracie gripped the parchment in her pocket. "Jacob said being in Bondoff could make us do things written in the story." She didn't add that Jacob had meant this as a warning. "Maybe it's the story glimmers leading me to Mom, showing me the way home. And telling you how to dress."

"But what if someone else is in the house? A different family could've moved in by now."

"We'll worry about that later." Gracie gripped the parchment tighter. She couldn't wait to see the house she'd been born in, to know where she came from—the thought made her almost giddy. She knew if she trusted her instincts, she would find it. Jacob hadn't mentioned anything about the confidence she'd feel in the story, the surety. She was strong, capable. The parchment warmed her hand; fear was being replaced by something else. Hope. Strength. The feeling that all her questions would be answered soon.

They entered the town carefully, sticking to the shadows between buildings, with the blanket-cloaks flapping about their feet. Gracie paused every few yards and closed her eyes, picturing the red house. The image grew clearer in her mind the closer they got. "I think it's a butcher shop," she said. "Who knew my parents were butchers?" Walter had given up arguing and followed mutely, checking over his shoulder as they walked.

Finally they found it, at the end of a dusty dirt road. The building was almost as she had envisioned, low and red, with a wooden sign that had a picture of a pig on it. One of the windows was boarded up. Gracie started up the front steps, but Walter pulled her back.

"We can't go in," he said. "We don't know who might be in there. What if Cassandra's inside? What if she knew you'd come here?"

"We'll go around back and look in a window," Gracie said.

They skirted the building. Beside the back door was a window that wasn't boarded up, though it was too high to reach. Candlelight burned behind it. Gracie scanned the yard for something to stand on. At the very edge of the yard, near a pile of heaping trash, was a wooden crate. She turned it upside down and stood on it to reach the window. The glass was grimy, but through it she could make out the figure of a woman on her hands and knees, scrubbing the floor. She brushed hair out of her eyes in a way Gracie recognized, and Gracie leapt from the crate so fast she fell to the ground and skinned her knee. She didn't even feel the pain as she jumped to her feet and flung herself through the door and into the woman's arms. "Gracie, wait!" Walter called, and she heard his footsteps thudding after her, but she ignored him.

"Mom!" she cried. In her haste, she knocked the scrubbing bucket over with her foot, and water soaked her shoes, but she didn't care. She'd been right to trust the story glimmers; they'd led her to Mom. She almost collapsed from the emotion of it all, and Mom stumbled backward under Gracie's weight. Mom was here, she'd found her, and as long as they were together, everything would be all right.

But Mom didn't return her hug, and when she'd regained her balance, her fingers pushed Gracie back, disentangling herself from Gracie's grasp.

"What are you doing here?" Mom's voice was cold.

"I came to find you! I—"

"Did Cassandra send you here?"

"Of course not. She doesn't even know I'm in the story now. She has Jacob, though, and—"

"What are you playing at?"

Gracie stepped back, squinting to see Mom's face in the gloom. Candlelight cast shadows over her cheeks. Her mouth was set in a harsh line, her eyes hard.

"What's the matter with you?" Gracie said.

"What's the matter with me?" Mom's voice rose until she was almost shrieking. "What's the matter with *me*? Why don't you go home to Cassandra and your father?"

Tears stung Gracie's eyes, and she reached for Mom's hand, but Mom tugged it away.

"Stop it!" Gracie was almost shouting now. "Do you know how much I went through to get here? Stop pretending! This is mean."

Even as she said the words, she knew her mother would never play a joke on her this cruel. Something was terribly wrong.

Tears ran down Mom's cheeks, but still she shoved Gracie and Walter out the door and into the darkness. "Leave," Mom said. "And don't come back. And tell Cassandra to stop this. Hasn't she taken enough from me already? Does she need to send you here to torment me too?"

And with that, she slammed the door, and Gracie heard the bolt slide into place.

13

Gracie pounded on the door and then the window, but Mom closed the curtains, and Gracie's shouts were met with silence. Gracie's whole body had gone cold and shaky, even her fingers and toes numb with hurt and panic. She couldn't see or hear or think of anything but Mom and the throbbing in her head that had started as soon as Mom spoke. Finally she became aware of Walter tugging on her elbow.

"Please, Gracie," Walter was saying. "You have to be quiet. We can't let anyone know we're here."

He pointed to the neighboring house, where a woman stood in the doorway, a baby on her hip.

"Go away!" Gracie shouted. The woman scurried inside. Gracie wiped her nose on the blanket-cloak and gulped back another sob. She shouldn't have yelled at the woman; it was only going to draw more attention and make things worse. She wondered where the words had come from. It wasn't like her to shout at people— her emotions were too high. Her palms stung from striking the door. She sank to the ground, resting her back on the side of the building. "My mom—" Her voice cracked.

"I know." Walter sat beside her.

"What do we do now?"

Walter patted her shoulder. "We'll look for my parents. Maybe they can explain what's going on."

"And what if they throw us out too? It was like my mom h-hated me." Gracie hiccupped. It was difficult to admit it aloud, that her own mother despised her.

Walter was silent for a moment. Finally he said, "I don't think she hates you. There has to be something else going on. Maybe it has to do with what Jacob told you about the story making people act funny. Maybe your mom's doing the things Gertrude Winters wrote about her."

Of course. Gracie had been so upset by Mom's behavior that she hadn't stopped to think about why Mom would say the things she had. "But why would Gertrude Winters write that my mom hates me?"

"I don't know. But maybe if we can get our parents out of the story, everything will go back to normal."

Gracie rested her head on Walter's shoulder. "I wish I knew what the story says about us. Then we would know why my mom . . ." Gracie's voice trailed off. "We'd know what to do."

"It's weird, though, isn't it? That she threw us out? I thought your mom and Jacob said we die in the story."

"We do."

"Your mom didn't act like the mother of someone who was dead, though, did she? When she threw us out?"

"No." Perhaps Cassandra had been telling the truth, that this was a lie. But why would Mom make that up? Gracie picked a stick off the ground and broke it into tiny pieces.

"Do you believe in parallel universes?" Walter asked.

"Like in the movies?"

"Like in quantum mechanics."

"What's that?"

"Quantum mechanics is a branch of physics that studies the smallest particles." Walter leaned against the building, his head tilted to look at the sky. "If you study particles at the absolute smallest level, the laws of physics are different. It's like the electrons exist in many places at once, and you have to catch them at the right moment to see them. Some scientists say it proves there are other dimensions."

"What does that have to do with anything?"

Walter turned. "At Jacob's house, you said maybe science could explain Bondoff. I was thinking if other dimensions did exist, that could be one hypothesis for where we are."

"So you think we're in another dimension where my mother hates me?" Gracie tossed the pieces of stick on the ground and wiped her hands on the blanket.

Walter was silent a moment. "Some scientists believe that if there are infinite universes, infinite dimensions, then anything you can ever imagine happening is occurring simultaneously in one of those dimensions. It could be this is a dimension where people act out the story Gertrude Winters wrote."

"But we don't know what happens in this story." Gracie took the parchment from her pocket. When she'd held it before, it seemed to strengthen the story glimmers, to guide her to her mother. She hoped it would give her more answers, tell her why Mom was so angry with her, but right now it did nothing more than make her fingers tingle. She handed it to Walter. "Close your eyes. See if it helps you figure out where your parents are. Maybe you'll see the glimmers too."

Walter looked at the sky, then at the parchment, then to the sky again, but finally he closed his eyes. The moon went behind a cloud, the shadows cast by the buildings long and thin. Next door, a baby cried. Gracie wished she were home having dinner with Mom. The air was turning brisk, and she pulled the scratchy blanket tighter around herself. Finally, after a long while, Walter said, "I think I know where to go."

༄༅

Walter's parents owned a shop down the street from Mom's butcher shop. A sign swung on a wooden post beside the door, but Gracie couldn't read it in the darkness.

"It's an apothecary," Walter said.

Gracie didn't ask him how he knew this.

Candlelight flickered cozily through the windows, and smoke curled from the chimney. Walter took a deep breath. "Maybe we should peek in the windows first, to make sure it's really them."

Before they could do this, though, the door swung open, and Audrey stood at the top of the stoop holding a lantern. She clutched her hand to her throat when she saw Gracie and Walter.

She was wearing a long, old-fashioned dress, but her nails were still painted dark, as they had been back at Gracie's house.

"Thomas!" she called, and Walter's father appeared in the doorway. Walter ran to them both. Walter's parents didn't acknowledge him, though, and instead kept their eyes on Gracie. Thomas bowed low, and when he nudged Audrey, she did the same.

"Your Highness, I hope our son wasn't bothering you. Please forgive him."

"Your Highness?" Gracie's knees felt rubbery. "I'm not—"

"She's right here!" Thomas shouted. Footsteps sounded from inside the house, and two tall men in boots and chain mail appeared behind Walter's parents, each holding a torch. One of them was thin with a nose that had a hump in it, the other chubby with ears like potatoes that stuck from the sides of his head. They both wore swords at their hips. Both bowed to Gracie.

"We told you she wasn't inside our house," Audrey said to the guards.

The thin one shrugged. "Queen Cassandra said she would show up here eventually."

Gracie edged slowly away. She should run, she knew it, but something was holding her here. They had called her "Your Highness." They had bowed. Who was she in this story? Was she really a princess like she'd always dreamed? Was she finally going to get some answers?

"Come along, Your Highness." The plump guard took Gracie by the elbow and steered her toward the road. "Queen Cassandra's been searching everywhere for you."

14

The castle was perched on a hill so steep Gracie and the guards had to walk almost vertically to reach it, until all three were out of breath. At the very top, invisible from the ground, a moat surrounded the castle on all sides. Shadows seemed to move within its depths, and Gracie squinted in the darkness and realized alligator heads poked up from the muck. One snapped its teeth at Gracie and started to climb the side of the ditch, but the plump guard kicked a loose rock at it, and it retreated into the water.

The castle was made of stone with torches mounted in the entryway, but only a few were lit, so the room was dim. More guards lined the walls, and they bowed to Gracie as she passed. Gracie followed her two guards up a staircase and down a long corridor carpeted in red and gold. The wallpaper showed prints of battle scenes, gruesome images of knights and ogres hacking one another with swords. The thin guard knocked once at a door at the end of the hall, and when a familiar male voice called, "Enter," swung it open.

Gracie almost couldn't believe her eyes. She was right—it was Jacob's voice she'd heard. He wasn't tied up or beaten or locked in a dungeon. No, he sat on a throne at the far end of the room, wearing fine cloth of burgundy and gold, with a thick gold crown on his head. His beard had been shaven—he was handsome—but he was still Jacob. And beside him sat Cassandra in a dress of the same color. She wore a crown like Jacob's, though hers was studded with jewels. Jacob clutched her hand. All around the room, in little dishes, burned bunches of sage and rosemary, and dozens of candles lit the room in a warm glow. Heavy perfume hung in the air.

"Welcome home," Cassandra said.

Jacob jumped from his throne. "Daughter! We've been waiting for you."

Something fluttered in Gracie's belly, hearing the word "daughter" spring from his lips: Cassandra had told the truth.

"Why didn't you tell me you were my father? You lied to me." The venom was missing from her words, though. Jacob looked so happy to see her, his mouth beaming, his expression so unlike Mom's had been when she saw Gracie.

Jacob's cheeks flared red. "What do you mean? When did I speak falsehoods?"

Cassandra rested a hand on Jacob's arm and pulled him gently back down until he was seated beside her again. She stroked the brown book in her lap. "Let me handle this, husband."

Jacob pressed Cassandra's fingers to his lips. "As you wish, my darling."

"He's not your husband," Gracie said, and Cassandra made a little choking sound. She descended from her throne and unpinned the blanket from Gracie's shoulders, tossing it to the floor and clicking her tongue against her teeth. "You really mustn't wear things like this, Gracie. It's beneath you."

Gracie glared at her. "What's wrong with my mom?"

"You went to see her?" The tight smile Cassandra had worn when Gracie entered had disappeared. She gestured to the guards. "Search her."

The guards' hands thrust roughly into Gracie's pockets, and the plump one pulled out the parchment and passed it to Cassandra. Gracie felt sick. Why hadn't she thought to hide the parchment before coming to the castle? Without it, she had no way out of the story.

Cassandra laughed. "At last." She opened her book and turned to a page where the center was jagged and torn. She laid the parchment inside, and Gracie could see where it had been ripped from it. The edges matched up perfectly. As Gracie watched, the Vademecum seemed to heal itself; the edges grew into one another, like skin closing over a wound. Cassandra ran her fingers over the healed page, as if waiting for something, but nothing happened. "Get Gertrude Winters," she said.

❧

Gertrude Winters still wore the same skirt and blouse she'd had on at the bookstore, though they were rumpled now, and stained, and her hair hung loose and messy. She looked much older than she had a few days before. Her eyes scanned the room as the guards led her in, and they froze on Gracie. "You're the girl from the bookstore," she said hoarsely.

"I told you I was telling the truth," Gracie said. "What did you write about me? Why's my mom so mad at me?"

"Hush," Cassandra said. She turned to Gertrude Winters and held out the Vademecum. "You said once all the characters had returned to Bondoff and the missing parchment was back inside, the words would be restored."

Gertrude Winters nodded and eased into a chair one of the guards brought for her. Cassandra opened the book to the middle. "The Vademecum has healed itself, but the pages remain blank. Why?"

Gertrude Winters gingerly touched one of the pages. She closed her eyes. "I don't know," she whispered.

"Well, something is wrong," Cassandra said. "The words haven't materialized, and Gracie is not acting the way she's supposed to. All the others resumed being themselves once they were back in Bondoff, and yet Gracie is insulting me and asking after her birth mother."

Gertrude Winters's eyes flicked to Gracie. "You said once the rest of the characters were back, you'd send me home."

Cassandra's face was squinty, and her voice held a note of warning. "Because you told me once they returned, everything would be the way it was written."

"I thought that's what would happen." Gertrude hugged her elbows across her chest. "I only wrote a story. I didn't ask for any of this. All I know is that girl made me sign a piece of paper in a restroom and I woke up here."

"I did not!" Gracie said. "I didn't make you sign anything!"

Gertrude Winters folded her hands and looked up at Cassandra imploringly. "Please send me home. Gracie just got here, yes? I'm sure she'll act more like herself soon."

Cassandra stiffened. "Jacob behaved the way he was supposed to right away. It didn't take him any time to remember his love for me."

Gertrude Winters gave Jacob a hard look. He shifted in his seat and wrapped his arm around Cassandra's shoulders. "I don't know about Jacob, Your Highness. But I have done all I said I would. Please let me go home. I beg you."

"Write the story again." Cassandra waved a hand in the air, and a guard appeared with an inkwell, quill, and small table. "And remember I'm watching you. Don't try any funny business. It should be exactly as it was."

"I told you, I don't remember the story perfectly," Gertrude Winters said. "I wrote it so long ago, and I never even published it. It was just—"

"If you ever want to leave here, I suggest you try very hard to remember." Cassandra held the Vademecum out on the table but didn't let go of it as Gertrude Winters dipped the quill in the inkwell. Gracie moved closer and watched over Winters's shoulder as she wrote. Cassandra glanced up at her but didn't send her away. Her face creased in concentration.

"Once upon a time," Gertrude Winters wrote, "in a land called Bondoff, in a castle on a hill . . ."

The quill scratched over parchment, and Gracie could barely contain her excitement and nervousness at finally getting to read the story—here at last would be the truth—but before Gertrude could write any more words, the ink seeped into the parchment and disappeared. Cassandra picked up the inkwell and dashed it at the wall. Ink spattered everywhere.

"I'm sorry," Gertrude Winters said. "I tried my best. I don't know why the words don't stay, but please let me go home."

Her face was sunken, and tears slid over her wrinkled cheeks. Gracie knew she should pity her, but she felt only fury that Gertrude Winters had written horrible things about her and couldn't even answer her questions. She was angry that the words had disappeared. She wished she had an inkwell to throw like Cassandra had done. Gracie looked up to find Cassandra's eyes on her, a slow smile creeping over her face. Gracie shoved her fists in her pockets and yanked her gaze away.

"Take her back to the tower," Queen Cassandra told the guards. She slammed the book shut and slipped it into the waistband of her dress. "And then clean up this mess. The king and I will tuck our daughter into bed."

15

Cassandra was silent as she escorted Gracie briskly down the hall, Jacob trailing close on Cassandra's heels and occasionally touching the folds of her dress. The castle was dank and drafty, full of corridors that twisted and turned so much Gracie wasn't sure if she'd be able to find her way out again. Finally Cassandra opened a heavy wooden door and gestured inside. "This is your room," she said. "I've had it waiting for you."

The room's stone walls were covered in tapestries, and brightly colored velvet rugs lay scattered on the floor. Oil lamps burned from bureaus and end tables, so the room was more brightly lit than the rest of the castle. The furniture was massive, dark mahogany, so even the wardrobe—slightly ajar to reveal a row of long dresses hung neatly—seemed imposing. A heavy scarlet quilt covered the bed, on which a tray of sandwiches and a pitcher of what smelled like hot cider waited. Gracie fell on the food immediately—despite her fear, she was famished and thirsty after her long day of walking; she couldn't remember the last time she'd eaten anything. It must've been at Jacob's camper, which seemed like a lifetime ago. Perhaps it *was* a different lifetime. This food was better than Jacob's cooking: the sandwiches were thick with ham, cheese, and butter, the cider warm and spicy.

"You asked who you are, and this is it. This is your room; these are your things. You are my stepdaughter, heir to the throne of Bondoff." Cassandra pulled a nightgown out of the wardrobe and laid it neatly on the bed. "When you are finished eating, you will wash and go to sleep." Cassandra gestured to a pitcher and washbowl on the bureau, her tone clipped. "Hopefully in the morning, you will be yourself again."

"What do you mean?" Gracie felt on edge, her heart racing, even as she swallowed a hunk of crusty bread. Everything was so confusing. She glanced at the brown leather Vademecum, still tucked into Cassandra's waistband. Cassandra rested her hand on it briefly, the way pregnant mothers sometimes stroked their stomachs.

"It's nothing to worry about," Cassandra said. "I'm sure it won't be long, and things will be right again."

Gracie turned to Jacob, who stood staring moonily at Cassandra and playing with a lock of Cassandra's hair that had fallen from its bun. "Jacob, is this what you were talking about at my house? That the story could make me do things, make me be someone else? I don't want to be someone else."

Jacob glanced at her, then quickly looked away. "I don't know what you're talking about. What do you mean, your house? You live here."

"Jacob, you know where I live, you told me not to come here! I'm sorry, but—"

Cassandra turned to Jacob. "Why don't you go to bed, and let Gracie and I speak alone."

Jacob hesitated, shifting from one foot to another, but finally he kissed Cassandra on the cheek, whispered "Goodnight," and ducked into the hall. Gracie watched his retreating back with alarm, frightened to be left alone with Cassandra.

Cassandra closed the door behind him and turned toward the bureau, taking a moment to examine her reflection in the mirror. She pulled a gold-edged hairbrush from a drawer. Gracie stumbled back as she approached, but Cassandra clenched her jaw and caught Gracie by the shoulders. Her hands were firm but gentle as she began combing Gracie's hair, easing through the tangles. Gracie froze. It was such a familiar gesture, motherly and painful all at once—Mom used to brush her hair when she was little.

"Do not confuse Jacob by talking about the past." Cassandra gathered Gracie's hair into a pile at the top of her head. "He has no memory of it. Neither does your mother, and soon neither will you. And then we can be happy again."

Gracie shook her head, and her hair slipped from Cassandra's fingers and fell loose about her shoulders. "I don't want to forget anything. I want to know what's going on. You promised you'd tell me the truth."

Cassandra sat on the bed and patted the mattress beside her. Gracie obeyed uneasily, her eyes never leaving Cassandra.

"Your parents lied to you." Cassandra's dress was starched so stiff it made a crinkling sound as she leaned toward Gracie. "I am not evil, and you do not die in the story. Your mother was upset about what Gertrude Winters's story said about her future—that's why she lied. Jacob loved me, and your mother was jealous. The Vademecum said that when you grew up, you would become my stepdaughter and you would love me more than her. She couldn't take it, and she made Jacob leave the story. That is all. She made you give this up, this power, this wealth, the opportunity to one day rule Bondoff with me, because she was jealous. What do you think of that?"

Gracie shook her head. "Mom wouldn't do that." She only half-believed the words.

Cassandra sighed. "When Jacob stole the page from the Vademecum, all the words disappeared. If they hadn't, I would let you read the story, and then you could see for yourself the extent you've been lied to."

"Then why did Walter and his family leave Bondoff?"

Cassandra wrapped her arm around Gracie's shoulders. Gracie stiffened. "How should I know why people do the things they do? Walter's parents are poor: perhaps they found out about the scheme and forced your mother to bring them along. Maybe they thought they could have better luck in a different place. Everyone is curious about my magic book, you see"—she patted the Vademecum lovingly—"but the outside world is not better than Bondoff. If it was, why would Gertrude Winters have needed to create this one?"

Did Mom really believe Gracie loved Cassandra more than her? If so, perhaps Gracie only needed to reassure her this wasn't true. Cassandra pulled Gracie closer until her head rested on her chest; she smelled musky, like flowery incense and lamp oil. "But why is everyone acting so strange? Why did my mom throw me out?"

"She's become her true self again. She's forgotten the time she spent in the outside world with you; it is as if none of that ever happened. She is back to the way she is supposed to be—the way Gertrude Winters wrote her. So is Jacob. And soon you will be too." She traced her fingers along Gracie's arm. "We'll be happy."

Gracie pulled away. "I don't want to forget my mom or my home or my . . ." Her chest tightened, as if all the air were being crushed from her lungs. "I won't. I've been in the story a whole day, and I haven't forgotten, and neither has Walter." Suddenly, she longed for Walter more than she'd ever thought possible. Was he the single person besides Gracie in this entire story who remembered being in the outside world? She felt terribly alone. "I want to see him," Gracie said. "I want to see Walter."

Gracie had thought Cassandra might be displeased by this, but she wasn't expecting the wide grin that broke across Cassandra's face. She smoothed Gracie's hair. "Of course you do." She frowned when Gracie shrank from her touch, but the smile quickly returned. "We'll fetch Walter here first thing in the morning. Now get some sleep."

Cassandra slid from the room, and Gracie heard a key turn in the door, realizing too late that she had been locked in.

16

When Gracie woke, sun shone through the window, and her door hung ajar. Someone had unlocked it in the night, and a fresh change of clothes waited on the chair: a pale-blue silk dress with gold trim. She sat up in bed, her heart pounding. For a moment, she had almost believed herself back at home. She'd had strange dreams in the night, but they were shadowy now; she couldn't remember what they were about, only that she had felt very angry. She remembered throwing something. She was surprised she'd been able to sleep at all—she'd lain awake most of the night, afraid to drift off in case she would forget who she was as Cassandra had suggested. She was relieved to find that Cassandra had been wrong.

Gracie washed her face and examined her reflection in the mirror. She still *looked* like herself; that hadn't changed at all. She hunted the floor for the clothes she'd taken off the night before. They were dirty, and she'd worn them for days, but at least they were hers. As much as she searched, though, she couldn't find them. Whoever had come in the night and laid the dress out for her must have taken them. Gracie swallowed hard, hoping they were merely in the laundry. Even worse than the missing clothing, she had tucked a photograph in the back pocket of her jeans, the one of Gracie and Mom, and she wished now she'd slept with it under her pillow. She would ask Cassandra for it.

It was either wear the blue dress or the nightgown she was in, and Gracie reluctantly slipped the dress over her head and examined herself in the mirror. She looked older dressed this way, and more like the other characters in the story. Something felt right about the dress, the way it slid against her skin, sweeping along the floor so that she felt grand, regal, beautiful. She looked at herself in the mirror for a long time, and used the gold brush to pin her hair behind her ears. Was this what she looked like in the story? She fingered the earrings scattered across the bureau and peeked in the drawers, which were filled with silk stockings and handkerchiefs. At the bottom of one drawer she found an embroidered purse stuffed with gold coins. The whole room was so unlike her bedroom at home. Would these all have been her things if she'd grown up in Bondoff?

Shortly after Gracie finished changing, a guard rapped on her door. "I'm to bring you to breakfast, Your Highness," he said.

She followed him downstairs and into the dining room, where Cassandra and Jacob sat at one end of a table so long it reminded Gracie of the ones in her school's cafeteria. It was covered in loaves of bread, muffins, jams, and sausages. Underneath a life-sized portrait of herself that hung on the wall, Cassandra calmly poured coffee from a carafe. In the painting, her lips were pursed, her hands folded as if in prayer and resting on the Vademecum; she seemed to sneer down at everyone in the dining room.

"How are you feeling?" Cassandra asked.

Gracie sat without answering. Jacob snuck peeks at her out of the corner of his eyes, as if watching for something, but he remained silent.

"I want my picture of Mom," Gracie said finally. "It was in my pants pocket."

"Out of the question," Cassandra said. "Have a pancake, dear." She passed Gracie a platter of cakes covered in syrup and butter, but Gracie didn't take it. Cassandra scowled. "What do you want it for anyway?"

"Because it's mine!"

"It's bad for you," Cassandra said. "Trust your father and me— we only want what's best for you. You don't want a reminder of that horrible woman, do you? Of all the lies she told you, stealing you away, forcing you to lead a fake life rather than your rightful one in Bondoff? The sooner you forget about her, the better."

Something flickered in Gracie's memory, a vision of Mom shouting at her, her face screwed up in fury. Gracie couldn't picture where this had taken place: was it a story glimmer, or had it actually happened in the real world? She wanted to slap Mom, to tell her to stop holding her back, to let her be who she was meant to be—Gracie took a deep breath and speared a sausage, anything to distract herself from the cold rage beginning to seep through her. She needed to talk to someone. She wished Jacob would be more help—Mom had seemed to trust him—but he was different here. And how well did Gracie know him, anyway? Even if he was her father, she'd only known him a few days, and he kept staring at Cassandra with that sappy look on his face. Even now, syrup was dripping off his fork and onto the tablecloth as he watched Cassandra sip her coffee.

"You said Walter could come this morning," Gracie said.

"And so he shall," Cassandra said. "But first I want to take you on a tour of our kingdom. It's time you were shown fully who you are."

🙰

The guards brought an open carriage round after breakfast, pulled by two shining black horses wearing bells that clanged in time to their hoofbeats. The morning was cool, and the horses' breath steamed. The guard with the hooked nose drove, and Gracie sat between Jacob and Cassandra on the bench behind him. On either side of the carriage, a line of three guards marched beside them, making Gracie feel enclosed, as if she were in the middle of a crowd. Cassandra kept patting Gracie's hand as they rode, as if to reassure herself Gracie was really there. Jacob was strangely silent, as he had been ever since Gracie arrived in Bondoff. She wondered if Jacob was quieter in the story than he had been in the real world, whether Gertrude Winters had written him that way, but she figured not because Cassandra kept glancing at him with a strange expression on her face and asking him if he felt all right.

"The reason I wanted to take you out today," Cassandra explained, as the horses eased their way down the steep hill, "is to give you a sense of the massive responsibility we share. Bondoff is a small kingdom, yes, but it is ours to govern, and you must be familiar with every inch of it if you hope to be a successful ruler. If we don't keep a close eye on the peasants, we could have insurrection, rebellion, chaos on our hands." They were taking a windier path than Gracie had done the previous day on foot, but all the same she was afraid the carriage would topple on its side. Cassandra pulled the Vademecum from beneath her lap robe. "Things used to be much simpler: when the words were still written in the book, I could trust that I knew what the commoners were doing because I knew what the story said about them. But now that the words are gone, I don't feel sure of anything. There is an old man in the village, for example. In Gertrude Winters's story, he was supposed to die two years ago. And yet, every time I go to the village, there he is! Still alive! So far, I have not remedied this, but we need to be vigilant. These are uncertain times."

"May I see it?" Gracie reached for the book, but Cassandra acted as if she didn't hear her and tucked the book back into her waistband.

"Perhaps once you are feeling more like your true self, you will already be familiar with the things I am about to show you," Cassandra said. "Or if we're lucky, perhaps touring the kingdom will refresh your memory."

Gracie stared out at the village as they approached it. She did not want to forget who she was, of course, but she was also not sorry to be on the carriage ride with Cassandra and Jacob exploring Bondoff. She had seen a bit of it yesterday with Walter, but then she'd been skulking in the darkness, afraid of being seen. Now she was able to ride openly and look around, for what did she have to fear? All her life she'd wanted to know what Bondoff was like, and here she was, getting a grand tour as ruler of it. How could her mother have kept this from her? How could her mother have hidden that she was royalty?

The peasants were already out, tending their shops, selling fruits and vegetables under awnings in the street. They bowed low as the carriage passed, their eyes locked on the ground. Conversations ceased as Gracie, Cassandra, and Jacob drew near, the din of market chatter replaced with silence. A toddler sat in the dirt by the side of the road playing with a toy soldier, and Gracie had a sudden vision of throwing an apple core at him and laughing when it struck him in the cheek. She shook her head as the child's mother scooped him up and hauled him away from the road, wondering why such a cruel image should have crossed her mind.

Cassandra pointed out shops and points of interest as they drove. She knew a great deal about the people of Bondoff, though they seemed to shrink from her and scurry indoors as the carriage passed. The funny thing was, the longer they drove, the more familiar these places and people seemed to Gracie as well. She found herself calling to mind the names of people in the street. The fishmonger, for example, who mopped fish scales from his front stoop, was named Albert, and she knew he had a son named Morgan who Gracie disliked because his eyes protruded in such a way that he looked like a bullfrog. When they passed a group of children skipping rope and singing a song about cockleshells, Gracie found she remembered the chorus, and she joined in until the children's mother herded them all into a nearby house and slammed the door.

She knew the streets and buildings, too, and even recalled the names of some of the occupants. When the driver turned down a side street, she recognized at once that they were on their way to Walter's. She craned her neck as they passed the butcher shop, but there was no sign of her mother. The carriage stopped in front of the apothecary, and when Gracie moved to get out, Cassandra laid a hand on her arm. "We stay here," Cassandra said. "Let them come to us."

The driver hopped from the carriage and banged on the door. Walter's parents hurried outside, Audrey hastily taking off an apron and smoothing her hair. "How may we help you, Your Majesties?" Thomas asked.

"We're here to see your son," Cassandra said.

Audrey frowned. "What do you need with Walter?"

"I think we'd rather speak to Walter about that," Cassandra said.

"He's not in, unfortunately," Thomas said. "He went to the forest to collect herbs for a tonic, but if there is something my wife and I can help you with—"

"No, that won't do," Jacob said. "Our daughter, Gracie, is eager to learn about medicine making—she's an inquisitive child, you know—and she asked to see Walter so he could teach her some of what he knows."

Gracie turned to Jacob, surprised he would make up this lie, but his face was earnest. "I don't want to make medicines," she said.

"Don't be silly, daughter. You've been talking about wanting to study with Walter for weeks." He glanced at Cassandra, and she smiled encouragingly.

"Trust your father, dear," Cassandra said. "His memory is better than yours."

"Do I make medicines in the story?" Gracie asked, but Cassandra seemed not to hear. She had turned her attention back to Walter's parents.

"I don't know that Walter will be able to offer much," Audrey said. "Perhaps my husband can—"

"Send Walter to us by suppertime." Cassandra motioned to the driver. "He'll spend the night at the castle as well."

Gracie thought she glimpsed a face peering through the butcher shop window, but before she could be certain, the driver clucked to the horses and they jolted away, Walter's parents staring after them.

17

At the castle, Gracie went straight to her room so she could be alone to think; the journey into town had left her rattled. How had she known who everyone was? It was almost as if she had two sets of memories and knowledge: she knew facts about Bondoff almost as well as she knew information about home. And which one truly was home? Her memories of life with Mom? Or the story glimmers of life ruling Bondoff with Jacob and Cassandra?

Walter arrived right before suppertime. Like Gracie, he had changed clothes, and he looked strange in a green tunic and brown wool pants, less like himself and more like the villagers Gracie had seen on the street, though he still wore the same glasses. He carried his backpack as well, which he set beside him at the table when he joined them in the dining room. His face was pale, and his eyes held a flat, tired look, as if he'd been reading for a long time.

Gracie jumped up to greet him, but he stiffened at her touch. "Good evening," he said, bowing. "My name is Walter. My parents said you wished to learn medicine?"

Gracie felt the way she had her first time on a roller coaster, as if her stomach was sinking through her body down to her feet. "You know that's not why I want you here."

Walter blinked. "I don't understand."

Cassandra laughed and clapped her hands. She smiled so wide, it looked as if the corners of her mouth must tear her cheeks. "Why doesn't everyone have a seat, and I'll explain to Walter what we require of him."

Gracie grabbed Walter by the elbow. "You remember, Walter? Right?" She'd counted on Walter; it never occurred to her he might change like Mom and Jacob—they were in this together, regardless of the differences between them; they had come into the story together. Gracie was the one who'd explained it all to him.

"I beg your pardon?" Walter said.

"Sit," Cassandra ordered.

Walter took the chair offered to him, an uneasy look on his face. He gulped his water and twisted his dinner napkin, as if not sure what to do with his hands. Gracie sat beside him, resisting the urge to shake him by the shoulders.

A servant brought in platters of roast beef and potatoes, but Gracie's appetite had dissolved. Walter, however, ate enthusiastically, cramming a dinner roll into his mouth.

"Gracie's hoping you can show her some of the herbs in the forest that have healing properties," Jacob said. "She's interested in making tonics."

"No, I'm not," Gracie said, but no one seemed to hear her.

Walter nodded. "I've been training with my father for several years now. He wants me to take charge of the shop eventually."

"If you don't remember, then why do you still have your backpack?" Gracie said.

"My what?" Walter spoke through a mouthful of potato.

"Your backpack." Gracie pointed, an edge in her voice. She felt as if everyone was playing a horrible joke on her.

"The satchel?" Walter's face wrinkled in confusion. "I don't know. I found it earlier today at my house. It's useful, though. I brought it along to carry my tools. I thought we might need them for your studies."

Gracie's head pounded, and she nudged her glass with her elbow so that its contents spilled in Walter's lap. It was as if her arm had moved of its own accord, but she smiled grimly, satisfied that she'd done it. Walter sprang to his feet, his chair clattering to the floor. A servant rushed over with a towel.

"Excellent," Queen Cassandra said, patting her book.

"I'm going to my room." Gracie thrust her chair back from the table and stomped off, ignoring the sound of Jacob's voice calling her back.

ॐ

Later that night, as Gracie sat alone on her bed, hugging her knees to her chest and looking out the window, she heard the sound of footsteps and voices as Cassandra and Jacob showed Walter to his room. She could judge by how close the voices were that Walter's room was a few doors down from her own, and she was comforted by his proximity, even if she was still angry with him for not being able to remember. She waited for Cassandra to lock her in her room again, but after Walter's door creaked closed, the sound of Cassandra and Jacob's footsteps disappeared down the hall without pausing in front of Gracie's door, and Gracie felt hopeful. After Jacob and Cassandra had gone to sleep, she would go to Walter and see if she could jog his memory. Surely he must recall something of their time in the outside world. Gracie remembered, after all. She fought her rising fury. Why was she alone in this? Why wasn't Walter strong enough to keep his memory like she had? Gracie lay back and stared at the ceiling. Her eyes felt heavy. She had to stay awake—she needed to talk to Walter. She'd only close her eyes for a moment. She began to dream. . . .

In her dream, she was a child again, no more than four. Her heart leapt as she recognized her house in the real world, the familiar objects of the living room, the television, the bookshelves, her favorite toys, the blanket she liked to curl up with folded over the back of the couch. Strange, that she should know that she was dreaming: when she was in the real world, she had dreamed of Bondoff, and when she was in Bondoff, she dreamed of the real world. But this dream wasn't frightening; everything was warm and safe. She hovered over the scene, as if she was floating outside her own body, watching everything from above. There was Mom, in the kitchen having coffee and doughnuts with Walter's parents. Gracie and Walter played on the living room floor. Gracie was building a castle with blocks she had managed to stack as high as her chest, and she was about to place her princess doll at the top.

like watching a movie. She worried she didn't know how to reconnect with her own body.

In her dream, the moon smoldered full and white as bone, giving the items in her Bondoff bedroom an otherworldly glow. Pine and wood smoke wafted through the open window, blowing tendrils of hair across Gracie's cheek. She brushed them away and padded barefoot to the nightstand, where a candle burned down to its nub. She lit a fresh one with the burning end and waited for the wick to catch before going to the doorway. Silence echoed.

Gracie's feet glided down the hall, her senses heightened more than usual in her dreams, though she still had a dull feeling of disconnect, as if her body was not her own and she was watching the scene unfold from a distance. She was, she knew, safe and sound in her warm bed, watching this other Gracie journey into the night, one hand clutching a candle, the other outstretched at her side, trailing its fingertips along the wallpaper.

Dream-Gracie knew which room Walter slept in, though real-Gracie had not watched him retire, and she opened the door soundlessly and stood at the foot of the bed, a gigantic thing, mahogany with a canopy and thin curtains that hung down, enclosing the sleeper. Gracie pulled the curtains aside. Walter lay on his back, his face pale in the moonlight. His glasses rested on the night table beside him, and he looked strangely naked without them. He made soft snoring sounds in time with the rise and fall of his chest.

Gracie watched as the dream-Gracie touched the lit candle to the bed curtains. Flames licked up their length. When the curtain had caught, Gracie touched the flame to the blankets as well. A fire burned low in the hearth, and she used the poker to scatter the glowing coals across the floor. The rug smoked. An oil lamp rested on the mantel, and though it was not lit, she tipped it on its side and dripped oil in a line across the floor.

"Gracie!"

She turned. Jacob stood in the doorway, his face haggard. He bolted into the room and took the wash pitcher from the bureau, flinging its contents at the burning bed and soaking Gracie's nightdress as well.

The smoke was thick. It billowed and burned Gracie's throat as she stood blinking, feeling suddenly awake as Jacob yanked the bed curtains down and beat out the flames.

Walter sat upright now, fumbling for his glasses, his mouth hanging open. "What's going on?" he said.

"An accident." Jacob crushed the curtains underfoot. "You left your candle lit, and it started a fire."

"I was sure I blew it out," Walter said.

"There's another guest room across the hall." Jacob yanked the blankets off him. "Go sleep in there, and I'll clean this up."

Walter eyed the drenched and smoking bedsheets uncertainly.

"Leave! Now!" Jacob said.

Walter scurried from the room, and Gracie looked down at the candle shaking in her hand, her dripping nightgown, and the embers on the floor, which Jacob was still stomping out.

This was not a dream.

Gracie set the candle down, her knees feeling like they might collapse under her. She swayed slightly and caught herself on the edge of the bureau.

"Wh-what happened?" she said.

"I told you not to come here!" Jacob rounded on her. The fire was out now, and he stomped toward her and shook her by the shoulders. "I told you that you couldn't manage it, that the story would make you do things! You shouldn't have come!"

Gracie stumbled back. "You remember?"

Jacob peeked into the hall and closed the door. "You must not tell." He was silent for a moment, and when he finally spoke it was in a hush. "If Cassandra thinks I'm the person Gertrude Winters created, then she trusts me, and she keeps me close, where I can help you and your mother. If she thought for a moment I didn't really love her, she'd lock me in her dungeon, and I'd be no use to anyone." His hand tightened on the knob. "It'd be wise for you to pretend too. You need to get to bed before you wake her. I'll take care of this mess."

Gracie surveyed the damage. "I was sleepwalking, I think. I don't know what happened. Why did I do this?"

"Go to bed," Jacob said.

A sickening realization was dawning on Gracie. "What happens in the story?"

Jacob cleaned soundlessly, using the wet bed curtains to mop ash from the floor.

"Mom told me I die in the story, but Cassandra said that's not true."

Jacob tossed the dirty curtains to the ground. "You weren't sleepwalking. It was the story's power acting on you, making you do the things Gertrude Winters wrote you would do. You have to fight harder against it. Don't you see why I told you not to come here? Your mother wasn't telling you the truth about the story glimmers."

"Then what *is* the truth, Jacob?" For the first time in her life, Gracie wasn't sure she wanted to know.

Jacob's hands hung limply at his sides. "You don't die in a fire; that's not what the visions were showing." He looked at her finally, his face appearing older and more tired than Gracie had ever seen it. "You're the villain of this story, Gracie. You're the one who kills Walter."

18

G racie hugged her arms across her chest. Soot clung to her skin, her hair, its bitterness on her tongue. Surely Jacob was lying.

Jacob's back was a brick wall as he hung the fire poker on its hook. "Go to your room. I'll clean the mess."

"But, Jacob—" Tears burned Gracie's eyes, and she caught the edge of his sleeve, leaving an ashy thumbprint. Jacob turned, his face softening. He rested his hand on her cheek, almost in the same way Mom did.

"Go back to bed," he said more gently. "I'll come talk to you when I'm finished."

Gracie slunk to her room. Her hands wouldn't stop shaking, and her teeth made a funny clicking sound. She almost laughed aloud when she realized they were chattering. You only ever read about chattering teeth in storybooks; it figured that her teeth would be chattering now that she was inside of one. There really was nothing funny about it, but the laughter threatened behind her clenched teeth; she felt as if she was losing her mind.

She peeled off her wet nightgown and kicked it under the bed, pulling on a dry one she found in the dresser. She climbed beneath the blankets, but her body still shivered and shuddered. Her mind raced furiously, recalling all the bad things she'd ever done: the time she'd struck Walter, every time she'd yelled at Mom, every time she'd let her temper get carried away, every time rage had seized her and she'd smelled the smoke. She wasn't the heroine in this story; she was the villain. It was no wonder Mom despised her now. Mom was kind and good, and Gracie was . . . No. She wouldn't let herself become a murderer. But how to stop it? She'd had no control in the dream.

Gracie's door creaked open, and Jacob stepped inside, closing the door softly behind him. As Gracie turned to look at him, she caught her reflection in the mirror and almost didn't recognize herself; her face was tight with fear.

"I'm sorry I spoke so harshly before," Jacob said. "I was frightened, and I lashed out at you. I shouldn't have thrown all of that on you like that."

"But it's true?" Gracie asked. "I'm a villain? Like Cassandra? Everyone is afraid of me?"

Jacob picked a comb off the dresser and ran his fingers over its teeth. "That's only what Gertrude Winters wrote about you, not who you are."

"But it is who I am!" Gracie bolted upright, and the blankets fell from her shoulders. "Look what I tried to do! I almost killed Walter! What if you hadn't stopped me?"

Jacob set the comb down and sat beside Gracie. A smear of ash streaked his cheek. "Back at my trailer, you told me your mother said we could be whoever we wanted to be, not just what Gertrude Winters wrote."

"What does Mom know? She lied to me! She told me I died in the story!"

"I think she couldn't bear to tell you the truth. She thought if she said you died, you wouldn't feel trapped by anything written about you—you could be yourself." Jacob tucked the blankets back around Gracie. "Your mother believed that by taking you out of the story, the villain part of you, the part Gertrude Winters wrote, truly was dead."

"Well, she was wrong, wasn't she? If you both had told me the truth, I never would have come here!" Gracie buried her face in her hands. "Mom hates me now. I tried to start Walter's room on fire! I'm a horrible person."

Jacob peeled her hands away from her face and wiped his thumb across her cheek. "You can be different from what Gertrude Winters wrote about you. You still remember the outside world. You don't have to let Winters dictate who you are."

"I'm forgetting all the time." Shame swept over her, making her want to curl up into herself, tighter and tighter, until she was no more than a speck of dust. "What if I can't control it? How do you remember?"

"I'm not sure, but I have a theory." Jacob's fingers traced the stubble along his cheek and chin, as if feeling for the beard that was no longer there. "I'm different from the person I was the day I took you and your mother out of Bondoff, but ever since I returned here, I feel the story pulling on me, guiding me more and more toward the way I was written. When I start to give in, that's when I become confused about what really happened and what are merely glimmers. I feel like if I don't let the story change me back, I can keep a sense of who I am, apart from what Gertrude Winters wrote about me. You can too."

This didn't make Gracie feel better. "I never read the story like you did. I don't ever know if I'm acting like myself or the person Gertrude Winters made up."

Jacob was silent for a long while. Finally he said, "You know the most important part: that the Gracie who Gertrude Winters created kills Walter in the story. You can stop yourself from doing that. You can watch your temper around him."

It hurt to ask; the very idea of what his answer contained made Gracie feel as if she'd shrivel into a shell of herself, but she knew she had to press the words out. It was safer to know. "How do I do it?"

Jacob looked very old as he answered. "You start a fire. Walter thinks he needs to destroy the Vademecum to defeat Cassandra, and you kill him in order to save it."

Gracie tensed at the word "destroy." Walter couldn't destroy the Vademecum; she needed it to get home. If she let him destroy it, she'd be trapped here forever. But no. She would not get angry with Walter ever again. Not even if he tried to destroy the book. The solution came over her in a rush. "*We* can steal the Vademecum. You and I. We'll run away again, and save everyone, like you did last time."

Jacob shook his head. "Do you think Cassandra's forgotten I stole from her? I may have convinced her that I've reverted to the way Winters wrote me, but she's not so foolish as to trust me with the book. She never lets me near it."

"*I'll* steal it then." Hope flickered in Gracie's chest, faint but sharp.

"It's not worth risking her anger, Gracie. She's dangerous, whatever she may seem to you right now." Jacob rubbed his temples, as if she were giving him a headache. "Her guards do all her bidding. She could throw you in the dungeon, or worse. Our best chance of protecting everyone is to pretend to be the way Gertrude Winters wrote us. Things are different now. I want to be a good father. I want to keep Cassandra from hurting people. And perhaps Walter's not in danger—you still remember your time in the world outside Bondoff."

"But I just tried to kill Walter without even knowing I was doing it!"

Jacob tugged at a loose thread on the blanket. "But you didn't kill him."

"And what about next time?"

"You know the truth now. Maybe there won't be a next time."

If Gracie hadn't been so terrified, she would have laughed at the absurdity. She fought the desire to slap Jacob, to kick and scream and tell him she hated that he was her father, hated he had abandoned her when she was a baby, hated that he wanted to let her down now. But she would not give in to her anger. She would not become a villain. She wiped her nose on her sleeve. "How did you steal the pages last time?"

Jacob pulled the thread harder until one of the quilt squares came loose at the corner. "I asked Cassandra for them. After she showed me what the Vademecum said about you, I waited for the right moment and pretended I needed something from the other world. A gift for her. She gave me the pages. Back then, it never occurred to her that I might betray her, that it was even a possibility I could betray her." Jacob looked up at Gracie, shame in his face. "It would never work again; I could never ask for it again."

19

The next morning, as Cassandra and Jacob prepared to take another ride through town to check on the peasants, Gracie pretended not to be feeling well and went to her room. She was supposed to be studying with Walter, but she didn't know if she trusted herself around him, and she had something much more important to do.

She waited until she saw Cassandra and Jacob leave through her bedroom window, and then she tiptoed down the hallway. Where was Gertrude Winters? The single time Gracie had seen the author here at the castle, she'd been heavily guarded. Cassandra had told the guards to take her back to the tower. But where was that? Gracie leaned against the wall and closed her eyes. Sometimes when she cleared her mind, like when she'd first arrived in the story and been searching for Mom, she knew information like where things were, or people's names in town. Relying on the glimmers was risky, she knew—the whole point was not to give in to the way things were in the story—but if the story knowledge could help her this once, to find Winters. .

. . Gracie took deep breaths and focused on the tower. She could picture the curving staircase, the stone-block walls. And then she saw the entrance to the tower in her mind's eye: the doorway was in Cassandra's bedroom. Gracie scurried down the hall.

Cassandra's bedroom was surprisingly feminine, with nearly every inch smothered in crimson velvet or lace. Mirrors and portraits of Cassandra decorated the walls. In some pictures she was alone; in others she posed beside Jacob and a baby in a lacy bonnet. Gracie examined the portrait closely. The bonnet looked terribly familiar. Was this the same bonnet as the one in Mom's trunk? Was the baby in the portrait her? Cassandra looked down at the baby lovingly.

"Can I help you, Princess?"

Gracie turned, her heart thudding. The hook-nosed guard stood in the doorway, an eyebrow arched into a question mark.

"I'm looking for Gertrude Winters."

"That's not a good idea, Your Highness. Queen Cassandra warned that the Winters woman's not to be trusted."

Gracie's head pounded, the familiar glimmering rage surfacing. She should fight the glimmers, but she needed this guard to do as she commanded, and there was something comforting in drawing on story-Gracie's strength. "How dare you question me?" She hoped he didn't hear her voice shake. "Take me to Gertrude Winters immediately."

The guard hesitated, but he eventually nodded and pulled aside a red damask curtain hanging from one wall, revealing a winding stone staircase. Gracie followed him up. At the top was a door, several inches thick, bolted from the outside. The guard took a key from the pouch at his waist and turned it in the lock. "Would you like me to come with you?" he asked. "Queen Cassandra said Gertrude Winters might be dangerous."

"I want to speak to her alone." Gracie made her voice steely. She needed to be alone with Gertrude Winters. Winters was her best chance at getting home, at making things right again.

"I'll wait right outside."

Gracie slipped into the tower room and closed the door behind her.

Gertrude Winters sat on a straw mattress. A half-eaten tray of food rested beside her. She scooted toward the wall as Gracie entered, her limbs folding as if she was trying to make herself shrink. Fear showed on her face, and Gracie felt as if she might vomit. Was Gracie really such a bad person that even Gertrude Winters, her creator, was terrified of her?

"Don't be afraid," Gracie said, forgetting for a moment why she was there.

Gertrude Winters didn't answer. Her hair was straggly, and she smelled sour and yeasty, her bony shoulders sharp against the corners of her stained blouse. She winced when Gracie reached for her, and Gracie withdrew her hand and fidgeted with the locket that hung on her neck. Cassandra had given it to her that morning.

"It's not my fault." Gracie's voice shook. "You wrote the story. You're the one responsible for this." Suddenly, Gracie understood why Mom had always hated Gertrude Winters. It was the powerlessness, the fear, that she hated, the sense of not being in control of her own life. Winters acted as if Gracie was a monster, but Winters was the one holding the cards.

Gracie could feel Gertrude Winters's eyes on her as she walked along the circular room. It was empty except for the mattress, the tray of food, a chamber pot, and a thin blanket. Through the tower's single tiny window, Gracie could see the village in the distance. She wondered what her mother was doing right now.

Gertrude Winters cleared her throat. "You sent me here. At the bookstore." Her voice was raspy, as if she hadn't spoken in a long time.

Gracie turned. "I didn't mean to. You're the one who wrote your name on the parchment."

"Please let me go home."

Gracie's heart sank. Could Winters really be that clueless? "You think I can send you home? Don't you think if I could, I would go home myself?"

Gertrude Winters flinched, and Gracie knew she was being harsh to the old woman, but she was too angry to care. Gertrude Winters had always been in control, and now she wanted to act as if Gracie was to blame.

Gertrude Winters rested her head on her arm. "What do you and Cassandra want with me? I already told Cassandra, there's nothing I can do. I have no special powers here, no matter if I wrote the story. I can't fix her book."

"Don't lump me in with her! I'm not at all like Cassandra!"

A flicker of interest sparked in Gertrude Winters's eyes. "Why are you here to see me then?"

"I want to know how to steal the Vademecum."

"What makes you think I'll know how? I told you: I don't even remember all of what I wrote."

"You don't remember writing that I was a killer? Making my mom hate me?"

For a moment, Gracie had hoped Gertrude would deny it, would say she hadn't written any of that, but Gertrude's face paled, and her mouth went slack, and Gracie knew it was the truth.

"You're making it sound worse than it was," Gertrude said. "I thought I was only writing a story! How could I know any of it would come true?"

The ashy stink of Gertrude's words made Gracie's head throb, and she gazed out the window and took deep breaths in an attempt to control her fury. "We are real people!" she said. "Not just your characters! You said yourself at the bookstore: all characters are real to the people who love them. My mom was right. What kind of a horrible person writes the terrible things you did? If you ask me, you're the villain, not me or Cassandra."

"But *you're* me!" Gertrude Winters caught a fold of Gracie's dress in her fingertips, urgency in her voice. "Don't you see? All of you—you're all me."

20

"I wrote the story during an awful time in my life." Gertrude Winters seemed to grow stronger as she talked; she sat up straight now, her body no longer bowed into itself like a comma. "Everyone I loved acted as if they despised me. I was tired of stories that only celebrated heroic characters. I'd done bad things, but who hasn't? We're not all good or bad. It's why I wanted to write a story that honored the villain."

Gracie sat on the floor at the author's feet, her anger cooling. Wasn't this what she'd always hoped for, to get answers from Winters? She'd never imagined it would happen like this, but Winters's words wove a spell around her. Gracie could listen to her forever.

"At the bookstore, you said villains were fascinating," Gracie said. "Your favorite characters."

"Because what does it mean, really, to be labeled a villain? No one actually thinks of herself as a villain. We are all the heroes in our own stories." Winters smoothed her skirt, tucking the edges behind her knees. "During the time I wrote this particular story, my daughter acted as if *I* was a villain: she felt I'd put my career before her. She wanted to live with my ex-husband and his new wife. I understand, you see, how all my characters feel. I understand how your mother feels, missing her daughter, because mine left me. I understand how Jacob feels, putting his own gain ahead of his family, because I'd done the same. Most of all, I understand Cassandra—she wants the certainty of knowing she'll get her happy ending, that she'll triumph in the end. Isn't that what we all want?"

Gracie stared at her hands. Wasn't that what she'd always desired, to know her story, one in which she was the heroine? It would mean she was special, important. "Did you write *me* so I was like you?"

Gertrude pulled a piece of straw from her mattress. "I wrote you very much like myself when I was younger: hot-tempered, imaginative, dreamy. That's why I wrote that you were obsessed with the story in Cassandra's book, because I was obsessed with stories too!" Gertrude chewed her lip, examining the straw in the sunlight. "But you're also a lot like my daughter. I was angry with her when she went to live with her father. I suppose that's why I wrote you the way I did—how you went bad after abandoning your real mother." Gertrude let the straw fall to the floor. "I'd made her out to be a villain in my mind, though now I think I was just angry with her. Perhaps I am the villain, as you say, as she said. She might never have left me if I'd paid more attention to her feelings."

Gracie folded her hands in her lap. The same thing had happened to her as had happened to Gertrude's daughter: Mom thought Gracie was a villain too. But that was too painful to linger on, and anger bubbled to the surface again. If Mom thought Gracie was bad, it was because of what Gertrude had written, what Gertrude had made Gracie do. "That's no reason to make me kill Walter. He didn't do anything wrong."

Gertrude drew her knees to her chest; something in the posture made her look almost like a little girl. "Walter is based on my ex-husband, so practical and logical. He doesn't understand the power of stories. He thinks they're a waste of time. My ex-husband used to accuse me of wasting time daydreaming, of living in my own little world. That was why I had you kill Walter in the story, you see?" Gertrude sighed. "None of it was real! How was I supposed to know I was making these things come true?"

"But Walter's not your ex-husband. It's not his fault the way you wrote him!"

"What good is a hero who fails to see a story's magic?" Gertrude rested her head against the wall. "You and Cassandra appreciate the power of stories, if nothing else. Walter thinks they're dangerous. He's likely scheming to steal the Vademecum as we speak."

"And when he tries, that's when I . . ." Gracie couldn't finish the sentence. The words "kill him" hung in the air unspoken, but Gertrude nodded as if Gracie had asked them aloud.

"But the Vademecum *is* dangerous," Gracie said.

"That's all a matter of perception," Gertrude said. "People have been thinking books were dangerous for centuries. They ban ones they're afraid of. Burn them, even. All books are powerful. The Vademecum simply has a little more magic than others."

Gracie pursed her lips, but curiosity won over anger. The Vademecum was the key home. "What kind of magic?"

Gertrude Winters smiled, a dreamy look on her face. "I don't think anyone's ever written of anything quite like the Vademecum; it's a clever creation on my part. Have you ever heard of a villain with the power to read her own story, to know what happens at the end? The ability to move into and out of the story world? The Vademecum makes Cassandra different from every other villain ever written. It gives her insight, instruction, and a way to bring about her own happily-ever-after. How I would have loved to have that for myself. A way to move into and out of my own story. A way to know how my life would turn out."

"But the words are gone," Gracie said. "The story's not written in the Vademecum anymore."

Gertrude tapped her lip thoughtfully "Yes, Cassandra is very worried about that, but I truly don't know the answer. My best guess is that something changed when Jacob fled the story. Once Jacob acted differently from the way I'd written him, the words disappeared. The Vademecum could no longer accurately predict what would happen."

"You think the story can change?"

Gertrude Winters wrinkled her forehead. "I think it's quite obvious it's already changed. That's why Cassandra's so desperate. It's not solely a matter of getting the words written onto the pages of the Vademecum. She needs the characters to act out those words to put the story back to right and guarantee her happily-ever-after. It's your ending, too. Not everything I wrote was bad. I didn't write that you grow old or die; once the events of the story have played out, you and Jacob and Cassandra live here happily forever."

Gracie's skin itched, and she scratched her arms, leaving red streaks. She wished she could climb out of herself, out of this character Gertrude Winters had created. "I'm going to steal the Vademecum like Jacob did. I won't do the things you wrote. That's why I came to see you: so you could tell me how to steal it."

Gertrude shook her head. "It's certainly possible for a character to do something different from what I wrote. Jacob proved that when he stole the page and took you from the story. I misjudged him; I didn't think deeply enough about what Jacob might do for the love of his child. But I don't think you'll change the story the way he did. Jacob is the only one who seems different from the way I imagined him, even if he puts up a good show pretending not to be."

"I'm different too. I still remember my time in the outside world."

Gertrude Winters patted Gracie's cheek. "Even when I met you at the bookstore, you were very similar to the way I wrote you. Your hair, your frown, the way you stick out your chin in that stubborn manner."

Gracie's palms grew hot. "I'm not the way you wrote me."

"Then why are you here right now?" Gertrude said. "Why are you with Cassandra instead of your mother? Maybe you prefer the castle."

"Mom sent me away!" The ashy smell had grown so strong Gracie moved nearer the window to gulp fresh air, though she knew it wouldn't help. The odor wasn't coming from the room; it stemmed from something within her.

"And so you gave up, just like that? I'm sorry, Gracie, but that is exactly the way I wrote you."

Black spots swam in front of Gracie's eyes, smoke creeping over her field of vision. Her dress stuck to her damp skin; she would not let the glimmers overtake her. "You're wrong," Gracie whispered.

Winters tilted her head in a knowing way. "Maybe." But she looked unconvinced.

Gracie banged on the door until the guard let her out, and then she fled.

21

Gracie flew from the castle, but her ribbon-laced slippers slowed her down, pinching her feet and giving her a blister. She stopped, untied them, and clutched them by their laces as she ran barefoot across the dewy grass. The sun warmed the top of her head as she gulped fresh clover air. It calmed her somewhat, reminding her of summer days at home before any of this had happened. She flung her arms out to her sides as she ran, her hair streaming behind her, dress skimming the ground, finally feeling free from the watching eyes of Cassandra, Jacob, and Gertrude Winters. What did Winters know anyway? She was just a spiteful old lady who wrote bad stories about people who made her mad. Mom was right to hate Gertrude Winters. She really was a horrible person. She could stay locked up forever for all Gracie cared. And so what if Gracie was at the castle with Cassandra? What was she supposed to do, beg her mother to take her in?

Yes, a nagging thought pestered. *That is exactly what you should do.*

If she went to her mother, she would be different from the character Gertrude Winters had written.

But, a different voice persisted, *if you abandon Cassandra, she will never trust you near the Vademecum. You'll never have a chance at stealing it and going home.*

The grassy hill behind the castle sloped to a wood at the bottom, and Gracie ran faster, pulled down by gravity and her own momentum, until she finally slowed as she neared the edge of the woods and paused only momentarily before entering.

It was at least ten degrees cooler in the shade of the trees. Gracie clutched a stitch in her side as she walked. A crow cawed in the distance. Pine needles jabbed the soft skin between her bare toes, and she brushed her feet clean and put her shoes back on. It felt wonderful to be alone, hidden among the trees. If everything failed, and she was never able to find a way out of Bondoff, could she live alone in the forest where she wouldn't hurt anyone? Perhaps she'd ask Jacob to build her a cottage out here. She stopped suddenly, and wondered if that was why Jacob had lived in a camper in the woods back home. She hadn't walked long when she heard a shy voice call her name.

She turned. Walter sat on a rock beneath a tree, his backpack at his feet. He held a magnifying glass and a small jar, into which he was putting some kind of leaves.

"I thought you weren't feeling well?" Walter said.

For a moment Gracie wasn't sure what he was talking about, and then she remembered she'd told everyone she was sick as her excuse for not being able to study with Walter. "I thought some fresh air might do me good," she said lamely. "What are you doing here?"

"Gathering herbs and roots for you," Walter said. "Willow bark is good for fevers."

There was something familiar about what he said, as if Gracie had heard him speak these words before. She felt lightheaded. She shouldn't be around Walter; it wasn't safe to be close to someone she was destined to kill. She wanted to flee, but her feet felt glued to the needle-strewn path.

"Come look," Walter said. "I'll teach you."

Gracie crouched beside him. He dug some kind of tubers from the base of the tree and sliced them with a small knife he took from his backpack. "Burdock root," he said.

"Where did you learn these things?" Gracie asked.

"My father." He placed the cork in the top of the flask. "He's been teaching me the apothecary trade since I was a baby." Walter shoved his glasses up on his nose and rocked back on his heels. The gesture was so familiar, so like the Walter she knew back home, that Gracie felt a pang like a dagger in her chest and was oddly comforted at the same time. This was Walter, still, but he was different.

Gracie placed her hand on his forearm. "You really don't remember?"

"Remember what?"

"You don't remember coming here? That this is all a story?"

"Are you feeling well, Your Highness? Perhaps you need some rest."

Gracie shook her head. "I can prove to you that this is a story. I know exactly what you're going to do." She thought of what Jacob and Gertrude Winters had told her about Walter. "You're planning to steal the Vademecum, aren't you?"

Walter dropped one of the glass jars he'd been holding. "Wh-why would you think that?"

"You don't have to be afraid," Gracie said. "I'm not mad about it." She swallowed hard, hoping this would remain true.

Walter knelt to pick up the jar. "I don't know what you're talking about."

"I want to steal the book, too." Gracie hadn't planned to reveal this to Walter, but now that she'd said the words, they felt right. Perhaps she and Walter could work together. Even if Walter didn't remember life outside Bondoff, didn't he and Gracie still want the same thing? In Gertrude Winters's story, Walter tried to steal the Vademecum. Now Gracie wanted to steal it. Why shouldn't they work together?

"Why do you want it?" Walter said.

"For the same reason you do. It's dangerous." She paused and added, "But we can't destroy it. We need it."

"You think it would be less dangerous for *you* to have it than Cassandra?"

"I want to use it to get out of here," Gracie said. "I want to go home. I want my mother."

"I thought Queen Cassandra was your mother," Walter said.

"I want my real mother."

Walter was silent, and Gracie rambled on. "If we worked together to take it, you could come with me. We'd use the book to get ourselves and our parents out of here."

"Where?"

"Home."

Walter raised his eyebrows, and Gracie corrected herself hurriedly. "Another place. Far from here. Far from Cassandra."

Walter stood and brushed dirt from the butt of his wool pants. He walked slowly, his eyes scanning the ground for herbs, but his face was scrunched in concentration. He opened and closed his mouth a few times before he said, "Did you have some kind of plan?"

"I thought you did," Gracie said. "That's what Gertrude Winters told me, that you already have a plan."

"Who's Gertrude Winters?"

"A woman who knows things," Gracie said.

Walter chewed his lip and seemed to consider something a moment before answering. "I wouldn't do anything to cross Cassandra," he said firmly.

"You don't trust me?" Gracie said. "But I can help you, I promise. We're friends."

Walter shook his head. "We better get back to the castle."

∾

Gracie couldn't remember a time when she'd ever been so tired in her life. She knew she couldn't go to sleep for fear of what she might do, or how she might wake up, and somehow, knowing that she dare not sleep made her want to sleep even more. Three restless nights had left her exhausted, and as she watched Jacob and Cassandra prepare for bed that evening, she summoned one of the servants to bring a pot of coffee to her room. She drank a cup, but it was horribly bitter; not even sugar and cream helped. Why did adults like to drink this stuff? She forced herself to finish the cup, and since she couldn't risk lighting a candle, she sat in the cool breeze and moonlight of the open window. The brisk air was bracing—perhaps it could keep her from drifting off.

Gracie's lack of sleep seemed to be playing tricks on her mind as well, making her fuzzyheaded and confused, as if she couldn't get her brain to focus clearly on anything.

In her former life—which was what Gracie was beginning to think of the time she'd spent in the real world with Mom—occasionally when she was very busy and stressed with school or hadn't slept enough, she would sometimes have the sensation that she couldn't quite remember what was real and what was a dream. It didn't happen often, but she remembered one time distinctly: a conversation with Mom about shopping for a Christmas gift for Gracie's teacher.

"But you told me you already bought her something," Gracie said.

"I did not," Mom said. "When did I say that?"

Gracie realized as she thought very hard to retrieve the memory that she couldn't puzzle out where Mom had said it. She had the memory of Mom's words, but she couldn't put the whole scene together: where she had spoken them, why they were there;

even the clothes they'd worn were fuzzy in her mind. "I wonder if I had a dream," Gracie said. "Isn't that weird?"

They'd laughed about it, and it hadn't been a big deal, but now Gracie was beginning to feel like that all the time, and it frightened her. She couldn't always sift out which of her memories were real and which were story glimmers. She worried she was losing her mind. When she tried to bring up a specific moment or image, she felt as if she was drowning, grasping underwater, her fingers flailing to catch the slippery memories that often as not slid through her hands. Sometimes she surfaced with a real memory: her fifth birthday party, for example, when she had dressed up as a princess but then eaten too much cake and thrown up all over her dress. But other times the only thing that would bob above water would be something she knew to be false, like an image of walking hand in hand between Jacob and Queen Cassandra, picking herbs and putting them in a basket. Skipping alongside Cassandra as she spied on the villagers, musing on which of them needed a visit from her guards. Kicking a dog who tried to jump up on her and snag fruit from her basket, laughing when it yelped and scurried away. The worst part was her fear that she might lose not only her memories, but her very soul, replaced by the monster Gertrude had written.

If Walter and Jacob weren't willing to help Gracie steal the book from Cassandra, she would do it herself. But until she figured out how, she needed to be careful; even as she pretended to be the story-Gracie to fool Cassandra, she could not lose sight of who she really was. She must not forget.

A stack of paper and a quill rested on top of the bureau, and Gracie sat cross-legged on the floor, the quill clutched in her hand like a rope for a drowning person. She would write down the things she knew to be true. She would write down everything she could remember about her life with Mom. She would hide it under her mattress, and she would read it every day, and she would not forget who she was. She hesitated for a moment before lighting a candle. She needed its glow to see by. She would blow it out if she began to feel sleepy. At the top, she wrote:

I am Gracie Freeman. I am twelve years old. I live in Wisconsin with my mom. Her name is Elizabeth. The two of us live in a tiny yellow house. I am not a villain.

Gracie paused, the quill poised over the paper. The floor was cold on the backs of her legs. What else did she know about herself? Her mind raced. Her time in that other world with Mom seemed so far away now, and the memories of it were becoming foggy, blurring together into visions of Bondoff. Her fingers shook. She could not think of anything she knew for sure about herself. She was not a villain. She would start with that. What was something nice she'd done? She must have done something kind for someone at some point. She tried to think of a time but could not. What about Mom? Surely Gracie had done something nice for Mom. But no, she'd been mad at Mom; she'd stolen Mom's parchment and gone behind her back to see Gertrude Winters. But the parchment wasn't Mom's anyway; it belonged to Cassandra. But that was wrong thinking, too. Gracie wasn't supposed to be on Cassandra's side.

22

The next morning, Gracie drank more coffee at breakfast. She would never get used to coffee's bitterness, but it made her feel more awake, even if it did leave her queasy. "You look ill," Cassandra said.

"Just tired," Gracie said. "I think I'll take a walk after breakfast."

"Is Walter not here?" Cassandra said. "I thought you were studying with him today."

"He said he needed to get some things from his father's shop," Jacob said.

Cassandra rested a hand on the Vademecum. "That is unacceptable. He is supposed to be here."

Gracie stirred sugar into her coffee. She must have scared him away yesterday when she told him she knew about his plan. "I'll fetch him on my walk," she said.

"We have servants for that," Cassandra said.

Gracie patted her hand. "Of course we do, Stepmother. But I'd like a walk. And if Walter and I are out together, he can show me herbs in the wood for healing."

Cassandra smiled. "Yes, all right," she said. "But don't be too long."

☙☙

Gracie's real reason for wanting to go was that she wanted to see Mom. Gertrude Winters had asked her about this yesterday, and it had bothered her ever since, that the Gracie Gertrude Winters had written would never go see Mom. She also hoped visiting Mom would jolt her memory, help her remember the things she had been unable to recall the night before.

As soon as she started on her way, though, she was forced to hunch over as blinding pain seared through her head, her heart, and her stomach. Her feet slowed as if they were wading through sludge. She felt as if an invisible force was acting against her, as if the story didn't want her to go. *I am not going to see Mom*, Gracie told herself. *I am going to spy on the villagers to make sure they aren't plotting against Cassandra.* If she truly focused on believing the words in her mind, believing that this was her reason for going to the village, the pain lessened, and she was able to place one foot in front of the other. It was tricky convincing herself that she was going to the village to spy on people; if she thought too hard about her true purpose, her feet froze, and she couldn't move. It was as if the story was stopping her from doing anything out of character. But twice when she thought about Mom, and how desperately she wanted to see her, she was able to shove the pain to the back of her mind, push past it, and keep walking. In this way, too, she was prevented from thinking too deeply about what would happen once she arrived at Mom's shop. Mom had already thrown her out once.

The village was busy this morning; some kind of market was going on, the streets clogged with carts and goats and men and women at tables, shadowed beneath overhangs, selling spices. The smell of cinnamon and cumin hung in the air among the barnlike scent of the livestock. Gracie skirted around them impatiently, but she realized quickly that the villagers were so frightened of her that they scattered out of her way as she strode through. She wondered if she should worry over their fright, but instead she felt relief that their fear kept them from slowing her progress as she made her way down the street.

She found the butcher shop again easily. Someone had applied a fresh coat of paint and taken the boards from the windows, which were scrubbed clean. Through one, Gracie saw Mom working at a counter, handing a customer a package wrapped in cheesecloth.

Gracie strode up the front steps and pushed open the door. The woman Mom had been waiting on made a little screeching noise in the back of her throat.

"Leave," Gracie said. The word flew from her mouth without thought. She had only felt irritation that the woman was there when Gracie wanted to be alone with Mom. The woman tossed a handful of coins on the counter and scurried from the shop before Gracie could apologize.

"What are you doing here, frightening my customers?" Mom didn't look at Gracie but instead busied herself tidying the shelves behind the counter. Gracie watched Mom's hands as she worked; they were small and slender, the nails cut short, with a small burn scar at the base of the thumb of the left one. They were hands that had soothed Gracie many times, had wiped away tears, held her when she was sad or frightened, combed her hair and cooked meals . . . and now Gracie wondered if they would ever touch her again.

"I wanted to see you," Gracie said. "I missed you."

Mom gave a forced laugh. "Why would you miss me?"

Gracie fought very hard to resist the two competing emotions within her. She didn't know if she wanted to cry or shout in anger, and this time, neither urge felt like the story controlling her. Both just felt like her. She knew doing either of these things would be foolish. She needed to remember that Mom believed Gracie had abandoned her. If Gracie had really done all the things Gertrude Winters had written, then she could understand Mom's anger. She was tempted to deny everything, but she suspected Mom would accuse her of shirking responsibility or shifting blame, so instead she said, "I'm sorry."

And it was true, she was sorry: sorry any of this had happened, sorry their lives had been destroyed, sorry she was no longer who she used to be.

Mom looked up. "Oh."

"I really do love you," Gracie said. "I know, with everything that's happened, it seems like I don't. But I do love you."

"What do you want from me?" Mom brushed a stray curl from her forehead. Her eyes were piercing.

"I want..." Gracie's mind went blank, and her tongue felt thick in her mouth. What did she want? She noticed for the first time the stickiness of the butcher shop floor, the counter splattered with blood from steaks, the buzzing flies that clustered and dove at her face and bit her arms. "I want to go home!" she said.

"Here?" Mom said. "You want to come here? When you could live at the castle?"

"No!" Gracie's heart beat fast, and she looked around wildly, feeling like the walls were closing in on her. Why wouldn't her mind focus? Where was home? Sweat broke out on the back of her neck, and her chest felt tight, as if she needed to concentrate very hard on filling her lungs with air. "This isn't home! I want to go to our real home, together. I'll steal Cassandra's book, and things will go back to normal. You remember our house? I promise, I'll do what you say from now on! You can make whatever kinds of food you want, and I'll never ask to see Gertrude Winters again, and I promise I won't look for the story anymore. I won't even ask you about Jacob. Or why you lied." The faster the words tumbled out, the sicker Gracie felt, and her head pounded until black spots swam in front of her eyes, and her stomach churned, the taste of bile rising in her throat. The headache was growing so bad she would throw up soon, but she must finish what she had to say.

"Why I lied? You think *I* lied?" Mom's face had been softening, but now her eyes flashed in anger.

"Never mind, it's not important. We'll get the book, and—"

"I think you should leave," Mom said. "You're unwell and saying things you don't mean."

"I'm not!" But words were failing Gracie, the pain in her head was blinding, and anger rushed over her, anger at the situation, at Gertrude for writing it, at Mom for not believing her, for not being strong enough to resist the story. She seized a glass jar from the shelf and hurled it at the wall. It shattered, spraying Mom with glass. One of the shards nicked Mom's arm, and blood beaded on her skin like tears. Gracie stepped back, pressing a hand to her mouth. "I'm sorry." The words were a whisper.

"Get out." Mom opened the door. "You've done enough damage for one day, I think." She seized Gracie by the elbow and propelled her out of the shop.

"I didn't mean to!" Gracie slipped down the two steps to the street, landing hard on her ankle. The tears came thick and fast as Mom slammed the door, and Gracie crouched in the dirt beside the shop and vomited into a bush. Her hair stuck to her forehead, and her head and throat ached from crying. She sobbed, not caring that people on the street were watching her, not caring about anything. Let them stare. She crumpled to the ground and hugged her knees to her chest. A hand pressed her shoulder.

She turned. Walter crouched beside her, rocking back on his heels, his eyes warm with concern. "Your Highness, are you all right? Can I help you?"

At that moment, Gracie didn't care that they were no longer friends, that Walter no longer remembered her. She didn't care if she was supposed to kill him. She clutched his shoulders and clung to him. "I want my mom. I want to go home. I don't want to be Cassandra's stepdaughter. I don't want to be the villain."

Walter patted her gingerly. "You were telling the truth the other day? About wanting to leave? You really want to go that badly?"

Gracie nodded. Snot dripped from her nose, and she wiped it on her sleeve. Her eyes felt puffy. She must look a mess. "Yes," she croaked.

Walter pulled away and looked her in the face. He took a handkerchief from his back pocket and handed it to her. "All right," Walter said. "Then let's do it together. I'll tell you my plan. We'll steal Cassandra's magic book."

23

"This is henbane," Walter said. They were walking in the woods behind the castle, and Walter pointed out a small plant with pointy green leaves and yellow flowers. "If brewed into a tea, it will make the drinker fall into a heavy sleep; they won't wake for hours. My father used it to put a man to sleep who needed surgery on his foot."

"You think it's as simple as getting Cassandra to sleep?" Gracie stared at the small plant. It looked harmless, not like the answer to all their problems.

"Not a normal sleep." Walter crouched beside the plant and fingered the leaves. "Once a person drinks it, they're dead to the world. They won't wake for anything until it wears off."

"Like anesthesia." Gracie had her tonsils out when she was younger, and the doctor had given her something so she would sleep through the operation. She'd breathed in some kind of gas, and before she knew it, she was awake and the surgery over—she'd slept through the whole thing.

"Like what?" Walter squinted up at her.

"Nothing." Gracie squatted beside him. "You're sure it'll work?"

Walter nodded. "I'll make the brew extra strong so we don't risk Cassandra waking early. Once Cassandra drinks it, it should give us enough time to steal her book, fetch our parents, and get far away. My biggest problem before was I didn't know how to get her alone or slip it into her food, but she trusts you."

Gracie nodded. She didn't mention that it might take some time to convince Mom to go with them. She'd worry about that when the time came.

"You still haven't told me where we'll go," Walter said.

Gracie examined him as he squatted beside the plant. Would Walter believe her if she explained about Gertrude's story and the world outside it? Probably not. "I know a place," she said.

Walter's forehead puckered. "You're sure she won't find us?"

Gracie squeezed his hand. "You can trust me. We'll be safe there. I promise."

Walter's eyes met hers, a searching look on his face. He must have been reassured by whatever he saw in her expression, because he squeezed her hand back. "Okay." He unzipped his backpack and pulled out a small spade. He dug around the base of the plant and pulled it out, roots and all. He wrapped the plant in burlap and set it gently inside his backpack. "I'll get busy right away."

"We should do it tonight," Gracie said.

"So soon?"

Gracie thought back to the way she'd lost control at her mother's shop and thrown the jar. She was exhausted—she couldn't stay awake much longer—but she didn't trust herself to sleep: what if she did something horrible again? "Yes," Gracie said. "Tonight. I'll put it into her wine after dinner."

⌇⌇

When they emerged from the woods, Gracie saw Jacob walking down the hill toward them. He sped up when he saw them, and Walter nodded to Gracie. "I better get started," he said. "I need to grind some more ingredients to mix with this."

Walter hurried toward the castle, and when Jacob caught up to Gracie he gave her a piercing look. "Why did Walter run off like that?" Jacob said.

"He had some things he needed to do," Gracie said.

"You're plotting something," Jacob said.

Gracie jerked her chin.

"Don't tell me you're plotting to steal Cassandra's book with Walter, Gracie! You can't!"

"Why do you care? You're too afraid to do it."

"Afraid? Maybe, and so should you be. I'm not foolish enough to try. I thought you had better sense than that. Walter tries to steal the book in the story. And when he does try, you kill him." Jacob seized Gracie by the shoulders. "If you plot to steal the Vademecum with Walter, you're doing exactly what the story wants you to do! It's a mistake. You shouldn't encourage him to steal it—you should convince him to leave it alone if you want him to live."

Something lurched in the bottom of Gracie's stomach, but she pushed the pang aside. "I have to steal the book. I won't kill him."

"What if you can't control it?" Jacob was nearly shouting now, his jaw hard. "What if I'm not around to stop you like I was the other night?"

Gracie's skin felt like it was on fire. She wrenched out of Jacob's grasp. "Stop telling me what to do!" she said. "I'm doing what you're too afraid to. And maybe you did stop me the other night, but that was the only time you've ever been there for me, my entire life! You abandoned me and Mom! And now you show up out of nowhere, and you expect me to trust you? You want me to give up everything and live happily with you and Cassandra and accept that Mom can't stand me?"

Jacob staggered back as if she had pushed him. "I told you I was sorry for what I did." His voice was low, cracking on the last word, but he cleared his throat and said more loudly, "Gertrude Winters was the one who wrote those things about me. It wasn't my fault."

"She wrote that you fell in love with Cassandra, maybe. But what about once we left Bondoff? When we were free of Cassandra and the story? Where were you then? Not with me and Mom."

"Gracie." He stepped forward as if he would reach for her, but she jerked away.

"And then, when you finally showed up at our house and brought me to your camper, you lied to me! You didn't tell me you were my father: you let me think you were someone else." Gracie's skin tingled; her entire body thrummed with anger.

Jacob closed his eyes and pressed his thumb to his temple. "You can't even imagine how much I wanted to be with both of you."

"Then why hide in the woods and lie?"

"I wasn't hiding. I was just . . ." Jacob's chest shuddered. "I was ashamed. And afraid of hurting you again. Of doing bad things like I did in Winters's story." His hands fell limply at his sides. "I thought maybe you'd be better off without me."

"You managed to hurt both of us pretty badly, anyway. Do you know Mom still cries out your name in her sleep?"

Jacob tried to take Gracie's hand, but she swatted him away.

"You're not my father, so don't try to pretend to be." Tears rushed to Gracie's eyes, and she dug her nails into her palms. She could have clawed his face and been happy to see the blood. Lightheadedness swept over her, and she had a sudden vision of whispering with Cassandra. Cassandra was handing her a red velvet purse. Bottles clanked together inside. Gracie pulled the cork from one and sniffed the contents. Lamp oil. "Walter thinks he is so clever, plotting to steal my book," Cassandra said. "You will set his room afire while he sleeps. We will never give him the chance."

Gracie laughed. "Of course, Stepmother," she said aloud.

Jacob scrunched up his face. "What did you say? Did you call me your mother?"

Gracie's eyes darted wildly. She was not in Cassandra's bedroom. She was outside, with Jacob leaning over her, a worried expression on her face. For a moment she had seen herself with Cassandra, plotting to kill Walter. But here she was on the hillside with Jacob, the sun shining, her feet sinking into the soft dirt. She had finally said the things she'd been feeling for a long time, but at what cost? Her anger had enabled her to say what she needed to, but her control was slipping away—she couldn't risk becoming the villain the story wanted her to be, not when she was so close to leaving.

"Leave me alone." She turned on her heel and fled before the rage overcame her again.

ণ্ড

Gracie paced Walter's room while he worked at his table. From his backpack, he'd pulled flasks of dried herbs and oils, and he crushed them with a mortar and pestle. He was explaining to Gracie what each one did, but her mind was too fuzzy to focus for any length of time. She was exhausted, but somehow her fatigue left her filled with nervous energy. She muttered to herself as she paced. The vision she'd had while yelling at Jacob was clearer than any she'd ever experienced while awake. It was like she'd actually been in Cassandra's bedroom scheming to kill Walter, rather than standing on the hill with Jacob. What if she started not being able to control her actions and speech when she was awake? Was Jacob right to warn her not to plot with Walter?

"Will you give it to her at dinner?" Walter said.

"What?" Gracie stopped pacing and turned to Walter. It took a moment to register that he'd asked a question, and she shook her head. "No, there are too many guards and servants around at dinner. Afterward, Cassandra likes to sit by the fire and have a glass of wine. I'll slip it into her drink then, when it's only Jacob, Cassandra, and me."

"You're sure you can get it into her drink without her seeing?"

Gracie nodded. "She trusts me." As she spoke the words, fear flared again. Cassandra did trust her. And Gracie was plotting to do something worse than she'd ever done before: drug someone and steal her most prized possession. That sounded like something a villain would do, but wasn't it justified by the fact that Gracie was doing it so she *wouldn't* become a villain like Cassandra? She wondered if she should allow Jacob to come with them too. Perhaps. Should she free Gertrude Winters as well? Or leave her in the tower to rot? After all, this was all her fault. *No.* Gracie dug her nails into her palms, disliking herself for the thought. She had to stop thinking like that. Of course she would allow Jacob and Gertrude Winters to come to the real world. Only a villain would leave them behind.

Walter poured the herb and oil mixture into a thumb-sized flask and handed it to Gracie. The mixture was a murky green color. Gracie puckered her lips. "You're sure she won't taste it?"

Walter shrugged. "If you put enough in the wine, by the time she tastes it, it will be too late. She'll fall asleep."

Gracie slipped the flask into the pocket of her dress. "You should stay away while I do this. Let me steal the book. I'll get you once she's asleep."

Walter narrowed his eyes. "Why?"

"I don't think it's a good idea for you to be there. If Cassandra caught you—"

"It's just as dangerous if she catches you. Besides, I can distract her while you put the potion in her drink."

"But—" Gracie didn't like to admit that she was nervous about allowing Walter to be there. But it did make sense for Walter to distract Cassandra while Gracie did what she had to. "All right," she finally said.

Walter nodded and cleaned up his instruments. Gracie turned away, unable to look at him. He had no idea that his greatest threat may not be Cassandra discovering him, but Gracie.

24

Dinner was mostly silent as Gracie, Cassandra, Jacob, and Walter gathered around the table. Gracie picked at her chicken, too nervous and tired to eat. She wished Walter would stop glancing at the Vademecum; he was going to give them away. Jacob spoke even less than usual, but Gracie didn't care if he was angry. When one of the servants came by with wine and water, Gracie asked him to bring coffee.

Cassandra raised her eyebrows. "Coffee? At this hour?"

Gracie looked at her plate. "I haven't been sleeping well."

"Perhaps you should go to bed after dinner," Cassandra said. "You're awfully pale."

"No!" Gracie nearly upset her water glass. "I'll be fine. I wanted to play a game of cards after dinner."

Cassandra smiled and patted her cheek. "Of course," she said. "But it's straight to bed after that. I don't want you getting sick."

"Maybe it would be better for her to go to bed now," Jacob said. He gave Gracie a hard look.

"I'm fine."

"Walter," Jacob said. "You don't look well either. You've hardly eaten anything. Would you like to be excused? Perhaps you need the night off. Would you like to go home to your family for the evening?"

Walter shook his head and shoveled chicken into his mouth. "I wouldn't want to go home now, not when Gracie and I are making such progress. She's an apt student."

Jacob scowled. Cassandra gave Jacob a searching look, her hand automatically going to the Vademecum and caressing its spine.

"Well, if everyone's finished," Cassandra said, rising from the table, "we'll move into the drawing room for wine and cards, I think."

As Gracie followed her out, her hand slipped into her pocket to finger the glass flask she held there. So long as Jacob stayed out of the way, Gracie might be back home within the hour.

ಬಬ

The night was chilly, and the servants had lit a fire in the hearth. Candles burned from sconces on the wall, but the room remained shadowy and dim. Cassandra rang a bell, and a servant appeared. "We'd like to play cards," she said. "Bring some, and an oil lamp so we have more light."

The four of them crowded around the table in the center of the room. Cassandra shuffled and dealt. Gracie picked up her cards; she had the queen of spades. It peered out of its one eye, seeming to glare at her, reminding her of Cassandra. *What are you planning to do to me?* it seemed to say.

Gracie discarded the queen and drew a new card. Cassandra sat across from her. She couldn't simply reach across the table and dump the henbane potion into her wine. Walter was seated at Cassandra's elbow; it would be much easier for him to slip her something. Gracie wished she had insisted he keep some of the potion as well. The oil lamp in the center of the table cast shadows around the room, but it also made everyone's faces seem warm and pink—even Cassandra looked friendly in the lamplight, as if they were a happy family playing cards at a table. Cassandra was smiling as she laid down a pair, Jacob patting her shoulder and joking affectionately with Walter. They could have been a family, Jacob and Cassandra the parents, Walter and Gracie the children. Except Walter was plotting against Cassandra, and Gracie was supposed to kill him. No, no that wasn't it. Gracie was the one with the flask; *she* was the one plotting. She jumped up from the table. "More wine, Stepmother?"

"That's very sweet of you, dear," Cassandra said. "Yes, please."

"There's no need for you to get it," Jacob said. "I can do it."

"I don't mind," Gracie said.

"I insist," Jacob said.

"I think it's your turn to deal, Your Highness." Walter handed Jacob the stack of cards.

Before Jacob could protest again, Gracie took Cassandra and Jacob's empty glasses and brought them to the sideboard at the other end of the room where the crystal decanter of wine waited. Gracie poured some into each glass. Her hands shook. She looked over her shoulder. Cassandra was talking to Walter, her back to Gracie. Gracie poured the sleeping potion into Cassandra's glass and swirled it around. She slipped the empty flask back into her pocket and returned to the table.

"Thank you, dear." Cassandra squeezed Gracie's arm. "I'm so happy to see you seem to be feeling more like yourself tonight. Didn't I tell you we'd be a happy family?"

Gracie smiled weakly and tried to ignore the way Jacob's eyes followed her back to her seat.

Gracie couldn't focus on the next round. Cassandra sipped from her wine glass and dabbed the corner of her mouth with a handkerchief. "I have terrible cards," she said.

Gracie waited for Cassandra's eyes to droop, her head to nod, but she seemed to be having no reaction to the potion whatsoever. Cassandra took another sip, and another, her hands skimming over the cards, her eyes bright and her neck erect. Gracie shuffled and dealt. Then Walter. Cassandra discarded a seven and drew from the pile. The wine glass rested at her elbow, nearly empty, the Vademecum next to it. Walter stared determinedly at the cards in his hand, not meeting Gracie's gaze. Why wasn't it working? Cassandra was only supposed to drink a small amount, and now she had nearly finished it, and still nothing was happening. Had Walter gotten it wrong? It would figure. He was always bragging about how smart he was, how much he knew about science, and then the one time Gracie needed him to actually put his knowledge to practical use, he'd failed. Gracie's head pounded. The lamplight flickered, and she imagined the lamp toppling on its side, the flame devouring the cards piled beside it. She stared at the tablecloth and tried to distract herself from thoughts of Walter, but it was difficult. If this didn't work tonight, what would she do? She couldn't spend another sleepless night. She had counted on being able to return home tonight, and the thought of needing to spend another night in her room fighting to stay awake was almost too much to bear. All because of Walter and his stupid ideas. She should have tried to steal the book herself. She should have known Walter was only showing off—

Gracie heard a crash, and she looked up to see Cassandra had fallen back in her chair. The glass at her elbow had toppled to the floor and shattered.

"Are you all right?" Jacob said.

"I feel ill," Cassandra said. Her skin was beginning to take on a greenish color. Out of the corner of her eye, Gracie saw Walter's hand snake toward the Vademecum. Her arm went numb, her wrist bumping against the table and knocking the book to the floor. What was happening? She had not meant to do that. As soon as she'd blocked Walter from the book, the feeling returned to her arm, and she crouched over Cassandra, pretending that she had only stumbled as she got up to assist her. This signified nothing. She would not lose control of her body. Her head throbbed. I am worried about my stepmother, she told herself. The pain faded to a dull ache. She took Cassandra's wrist in her hand.

"Are you all right, Stepmother?" she said. The words tumbled out of her mouth— she'd had no intention of saying them. It was as if her body was not her own.

Cassandra moaned. "I feel so weak. And my head." Cassandra placed a finger on her temple, wincing.

Jacob turned to Gracie. "What did you put in the wine?"

Gracie didn't answer.

"Gracie wouldn't put something in the wine," Cassandra whispered, but her voice shook.

"I have it," Walter said from behind Gracie. "I have the book, Gracie."

Gracie turned. Walter hugged the Vademecum to his chest. A smile spread across his face, and his cheeks puffed out in a pompous way. "We did it."

Cassandra snagged Gracie's hand. "You did this?"

"No," Gracie said automatically.

"But, Gracie—" A note of fear echoed in Walter's voice.

Jacob turned to Gracie. "You were a part of this?"

Had she done it? Gracie tried to say the word 'yes,' but the inside of her mouth was dry, her tongue swollen and sticky. "No," she said again.

"Yes, you were." Walter's eyes were huge behind his glasses, and they darted to the book in his hands. "Please, Gracie, this was your idea."

Jacob placed a hand on Walter's shoulder. "Don't worry— you're not in trouble. And anyway, it's done now, no matter whose idea it was."

Gracie glared at Walter. He clutched the book to his chest, a self-important look on his face as he held the stolen property, something that was rightfully Gracie's.

Cassandra reached feebly for the book. "Guards!" she tried to shout, but the word came out a rasping whisper.

Jacob ran a hand over his hair and took a breath. "We should go. We'll let Gertrude Winters out of the tower, and then we'll go find your mother and Walter's parents."

"Who said anything about Gertrude Winters?" Gracie said. "Or you, for that matter?" She didn't hear Jacob's reply, though, because she was too focused on Cassandra. There was a rattle in Cassandra's chest now, and her breast heaved as if each breath was an effort. She slouched onto Jacob, and Jacob gently lowered her to the floor so she was lying on her back.

"What's wrong with her?" Gracie said. She rounded on Walter. "You said the potion was just supposed to make her sleep."

"It was!" Walter said. "When my dad used it on one of his patients, that's all it did."

"You made it the same way?"

Walter nodded. "I gave her a little more to make sure she'd sleep, but otherwise I made it exactly the same. I didn't think she'd drink the whole glass."

Cassandra's eyelashes fluttered on her cheeks. She didn't look threatening now, so weak and helpless on the floor. What was it Gertrude Winters had said about Cassandra and Gracie? That they both had the desire to be the heroines of their own story, that they both appreciated the magic of stories in a way Walter never could.

"Can you fix her?"

Walter's voice was shrill. "I don't know. I have some herbs in my room I could try."

"Go get them," Gracie said.

"Gracie, we have to go now," Jacob said. "It's our only chance to get out of here."

"We can't leave her like this," Gracie said. "I think she's dying."

She turned to Walter, who stood rooted to the floor. "Why aren't you moving? Get them! Now!"

Walter took off, the book still clutched to his chest.

"This is what I warned you about," Jacob said. "Don't get angry at Walter, Gracie."

"I'm not getting angry at him. I don't want to kill anybody, and I won't be responsible for Cassandra's murder. Go find my mom and Walter's parents. Bring them back here. Walter's father is like a doctor, right? He can fix Cassandra, and then we'll leave. Walter has the book now."

"Maybe Walter should get them," Jacob said. "I don't think it's a good idea to leave you alone with him."

"I need Walter here," Gracie said. "I need him to try to heal Cassandra. And I'm not leaving her either. Mom probably wouldn't come if she saw me. If she won't go with you, make her. Pick her up and carry her if you have to, but hurry. The sooner you get them and come back, the sooner we can leave."

Jacob looked over his shoulder uncertainly, but he finally did as Gracie asked, closing the door softly behind him.

25

Cassandra drifted in and out of consciousness, and Gracie sat on the floor beside her, holding her hand so she could feel for the faint pulse in her wrist. What was taking Walter so long? Cassandra would be dead before Walter came back with his herbs.

Gracie had tried so hard not to become the person Gertrude Winters had written. She'd thought she was fighting it, but here she was, about to be able to go home, and even though she hadn't hurt Walter, she might have killed Cassandra. Was there no escape? Was she destined to be a murderer no matter what she did? She'd have to spend her entire life hiding, like Jacob, staying away from people so she didn't hurt anyone. Where was Walter?

Finally the door eased open, and Walter appeared wearing his backpack. "It's about time!" Gracie shouted.

"I had to grind the herbs," Walter said. "Otherwise she couldn't drink them."

He took a fresh glass of wine from the sideboard and mixed the herbs with it. They tried to pour it down Cassandra's throat, but it spilled down her chin.

Gracie shook Cassandra. "You've got to wake up. You need to drink this."

Cassandra's eyes fluttered open, and Gracie propped her into a seated position.

"You have to try harder," Gracie said. "I'm sorry. Walter said it would only make you sleep. I just wanted to go home."

Cassandra's mouth moved as if she was trying to speak, but the sound was so quiet, Gracie couldn't make out the words. She leaned closer until Cassandra's breath tickled her ear.

"Walter lies," Cassandra said. "He always intended to murder me. He used you to help him do it. He fooled you. Walter is our enemy in the story; if you had read it, you would know."

Gracie looked up at Walter. He was still standing there with his backpack, Cassandra's book in his arms. He didn't look at all worried about Cassandra. What did the story say about Walter?

"What should I do?" Gracie asked Cassandra, but as she said the words, she knew she didn't really need to ask. The lamp burned cheerily on the table. Its bottom was filled to the brim with oil; its flame flickered orange and friendly. She had always known, for as long as she could remember, that fire was her destiny. Her entire body felt warm, all the way down to her toes, as if she were curled inside a snug blanket. With the heat came a feeling of dreamy surrender: she could no longer control the movement of her limbs, but this didn't worry her the way she expected it to. "Give me the book," Gracie said.

"What?" Walter looked puzzled.

Gracie held out a hand for it. "I need to see it."

Walter handed it to her. Gracie thumbed through the pages. The words were starting to return. This was what she had waited for, the opportunity to read her story, but she didn't need the words anymore, and she closed the Vademecum and slipped it into the waistband of her dress. She knew what the story said she must do. She always knew what happened at the end.

Walter had lied to her. He'd told her Cassandra would only sleep, but he knew all along it would kill her. Walter moved to the opposite end of the room and mixed something with his mortar and pestle. His movements were twitchy, and a container of herbs spilled on the floor. He wouldn't try to heal Cassandra. It was all show. He was only pretending. Gracie picked up the lamp. It was heavy and warm in her hand. She looked down at Cassandra, eyes closed on the floor beside her. She was dying, and Walter had ensured it would be Gracie's fault. Cassandra was the only one who had ever told Gracie the truth about the story—perhaps because she was the only one who valued their story as much as Gracie did. If Walter could so thoughtlessly kill off Cassandra, whose character in the story was so similar to Gracie's own, would Walter go after Gracie too? Would he try to take the book from Gracie next?

Gracie's thoughts jumbled, as if her mind was filled with smoke, so that she couldn't separate one idea from another. At one moment, she felt as if she were back home with Mom, then she was here in this room, then she was in a fire, then she was crying, then Mom was telling her to get out and she was throwing the jar at her.

But it wasn't a jar in Gracie's hand; it was the lit lamp that she hurled at Walter.

She missed, and the lamp smashed on the floor several feet from her target, spewing oil and flame. The blaze blasted heat and sucked the oxygen from the air, erupting into a wall of fire that cut the room in half, leaving Gracie and Cassandra on one side, with the door and the safety of the hallway, and Walter on the other side of the flames, trapped between the fire and the wall.

"What are you doing?!" Walter shouted.

The door burst open behind Gracie, and Jacob plunged into the room, followed by Mom, Walter's parents, and Gertrude Winters.

As soon as Gracie saw Mom, her head cleared. This was her real mother, not Cassandra. But Mom didn't love Gracie anymore. Cassandra understood the bad parts inside of Gracie. She wanted Gracie in spite of the bad things she did. Or was it because of the bad parts she shared with Gracie?

"Gracie, stop!" Mom grabbed Gracie by the wrist. Once again, she was trying to save Gracie from herself, but there was no tenderness etched in Mom's face, only anger. Perhaps Mom was trying to protect Walter now, not Gracie. Mom had always known Gracie was a murderer. Maybe she was sorry to have her as a daughter. Was this why Jacob left? Because no one wanted to be the parent of someone like her?

Walter screamed for help, coughing on the smoke that strangled him. His parents dashed toward him, but the flames drove them back. Gracie's eyes burned and wept. She had proven everyone right—she was as bad as they all thought. She had started the fire that would kill Walter. The blaze was consuming the room; surely there wasn't much time.

Walter's screams became more desperate, and Gracie wrenched her hand free, but Mom caught her by the arm again.

"No!" Mom shouted. Did fear flash on her face too, or was it the flames playing tricks on Gracie's eyes?

"He needs my help!" Gracie said, but Mom's grip remained tight on her arm, hauling her away from the fire.

Mom was trying to protect Gracie again, even if she had no memory of their time in the outside world. But she couldn't save Gracie from herself anymore. Gracie had to do that on her own. She would go through the flames even if it meant risking her own life: there were worse things than dying. Mom knew that—it was why she'd told Gracie she died in the story rather than confess Gracie was a murderer.

She twisted free of Mom's grasp and lunged for the window, tearing the heavy curtains from their rod. The thick drapery weighed on her arms, but she gritted her teeth and raised her arms again and again, beating the flames and plunging into the blaze.

The sickening stench of scorching hair and charring fabric, the ash on her tongue, the smoke scalding her lungs and forcing her eyes into watery slits—it was the worst of the story glimmers, no longer the shadows of nightmares, but hellish and deadly. Perhaps the story Mom had told Gracie would come true after all: perhaps Gracie would die.

Then Mom and Jacob were beside her. Through streaming eyes and swirling smoke, she saw them beating the flames with rugs. The fire writhed and hissed, but Gracie's parents bucked and swayed side-by-side. A spark caught the hem of Mom's dress, and Jacob stamped it out. As Gracie reached Walter, the air crackled, the heat so intense that she was sure she wouldn't make it, but strong arms braced her as she snagged the strap of his backpack. The arms carried Gracie and Walter through, and she saw only the faces of her parents, red with heat and strain, before she collapsed beside them on the floor. Whatever they thought of Gracie, they were here with her now.

ᘏᘓ

The fire was out. The floorboards were blackened, the walls scorched, but they locked themselves in the drawing room. Guards banged on the door, drawn by the smell, despite the fact that Jacob and Gracie both ordered them away. Smoke hung heavy in the air, and everything stunk of ash. Cassandra lay on the floor unconscious, her breaths growing weaker and further apart. Thomas knelt over her with his medicine bag. Gertrude sat beside him, stroking Cassandra's hair. Walter rested in Audrey's arms, his skin black with soot but unburned. Gracie couldn't bring herself to look at him. She was too ashamed. She hung back, away from the others.

"We have to leave, now," Jacob said. "The lock won't hold forever."

"This is nonsense," Audrey said. "How could there be another world besides this one?"

"It's true," Gertrude Winters said.

"I don't understand." Mom wrung her hands. "None of this makes sense. How can this all be a story? This is our life."

Jacob knelt before Mom and took her hands in his. "I was a terrible husband and a terrible father," he said. "You deserve better, and if you wish, after this night, I will leave you both alone forever. But you must trust me on this. Let me make things right. Let me get you out."

Gracie wondered if these were the same words he'd spoken twelve years ago.

Mom's face was pained, but she didn't pull away from Jacob's touch. "I don't know that I can believe this. How can I?" She gestured to Gertrude Winters. "How can I accept that the things some woman wrote about us came true?"

Gracie pulled the Vademecum from her waistband and brushed the ash from it. She brought it to Mom. "Touch it," she said. "You'll be able to feel its power. I know it's hard to believe, but we had a different life than this one. It wasn't perfect, but we were together, and we loved each other. Please give me a chance."

Mom's eyes were watery. She pushed the book away. At first Gracie thought Mom was rejecting her again, but then Mom said, "I saw the way you tried to save Walter. I don't need a book to tell me how to feel about you."

Tears ran down Gracie's cheeks, and Mom wiped them away.

"We live together in this other world?" Mom said. "And we'll be safe from Cassandra? That sounds too good to be true."

"Like some kind of fairy tale," Gracie said.

The pounding on the door took on a new tone—it sounded as if the guards were ramming it with something heavy. Jacob pushed the table in front of the door and stacked two chairs on top. "We don't have long," he said.

Thomas stumbled to his feet, looking down at Cassandra and wagging his head. "I can't save her. I don't know what to do. It's dangerous to use that much of the sleeping potion. Walter was foolish to do so."

Walter stared at the ground.

"She really was one of my most fascinating characters," Gertrude said sadly. "The villains always are."

Gracie leaned over Cassandra. Her face was ashen. Gracie hadn't killed Walter, but she was still going to be a murderer. Cassandra was going to die, and it was her fault.

Gracie turned to Mom. "I need you to know I love you," she said. "You're my mother, my only mother. If you could remember the way things were before, in the outside world, you would know that. But right now, I need you to trust me. We need to leave, but I want to bring Cassandra with us."

The Vademecum grew warm in Gracie's hand, and she wiped her palm on her dress, trying not to think about whether this had meaning. It didn't matter. Gracie was deciding for herself what she needed to do. Only . . . she wished Mom didn't look so sad.

"She hunted us down last time!" Jacob sputtered. "This is our chance to escape her for good."

"You heard Thomas. If we leave her here, she's going to die. If we bring her with us, we can take her to a hospital. I don't know if modern medicine can save her, but she at least has a better chance than if we leave her here."

"She's evil," Audrey said.

Mom didn't say anything. She stared at her hands, a hurt look on her face, and this was perhaps the most difficult response of all.

"But I was evil in the story, too!" Gracie said. "That's what Gertrude Winters wrote. And if my mom and Jacob hadn't taken me out of the story, I'd probably still be evil. What if Cassandra's only evil because she never had the chances I did? She never got to grow up outside of the story where she could make her own choices."

"Cassandra will try to get the Vademecum again," Gertrude said. "It's how I wrote her. She's obsessed with it."

"You don't know how Cassandra will act in the real world," Gracie said. "You don't control things there. If we need to, we can send her back to Bondoff once she's well. But she deserves a chance."

Gracie opened the Vademecum to the first page. The words were thick together now, but she didn't want to read them. She didn't need to read what the story said about her. Only she would control what she did.

The book started to glow, pulsing beneath her hands. Gracie unhooked the string of gold pencils from Cassandra's waist.

"Everyone needs to be touching the book." Gracie grabbed Cassandra's hand and pressed her fingers to the page. The others gathered in a circle around her.

Gracie wrote each person's name in the Vademecum, and as she felt its power start to work on her, as the familiar tugging behind her belly button grew stronger, she glimpsed the top line of the first page. It no longer said, "Once in a land called Bondoff, in a castle on a hill." Instead it read, "Once, long ago, a butcher and his wife took their baby girl Gracie and fled the land of Bondoff."

It was different now. Gracie had changed the story. And then everything went black.

Gracie woke in a hospital. Mom sat in a chair beside her bed wearing a hospital gown and a robe. Her hair was pulled into a ponytail. Gracie sat up. A plastic bracelet with her name printed on it circled her wrist, and a hospital gown covered her shoulders. "What am I doing here?" Gracie said.

"Just a precaution," Mom said. "The doctors said you were exhausted from lack of sleep and stress."

"You remember?" Tears sprang to Gracie's eyes, and Mom jumped out of her chair and settled on the bed beside Gracie, wrapping an arm around her.

"I remembered as soon as we got back to the real world. I'm so sorry, Gracie. It's like the whole time we were in Bondoff, I was living in a fog. I think a part of me still remembered this world—I'd have flashes in my dreams—but then I'd wake up, and you'd be living at the castle with Cassandra. . . ." Mom was silent a moment. "It was like the more I loved you, the harder it was to remember."

Gracie nodded. "I didn't know how bad it would be there. I never should've tried to find Gertrude Winters. I should've trusted you."

Mom shook her head. "No, I shouldn't have lied to you. If I hadn't been so secretive, you wouldn't have needed to go searching for answers. I should've realized you were old enough to handle the truth about what that Winters woman wrote. It didn't matter anyway; you weren't the person she wrote about."

"You don't think I acted like a villain?"

Mom smiled. "Of course not."

"I thought that's why you didn't want me to know. Because you were afraid I'd hurt someone."

"I didn't tell you because I didn't want you to believe that about yourself, Gracie. Not because I thought it was true." Mom tucked Gracie's hair behind her ear.

"But Gertrude said I acted the way she wrote me."

"I don't care what that woman says." Mom screwed up her mouth, and Gracie knew she still hadn't forgiven Gertrude. "She doesn't know you better than your own mother. And besides, you proved that wasn't true last night, didn't you? You saved Walter and Cassandra."

"Cassandra's not dead?" Gracie had been afraid to ask this, afraid she'd find she was a murderer after all, but Mom shook her head.

"She's alive, just sleeping. The doctors say she's going to make a full recovery. They did have questions about why she drank henbane. I had to tell the doctors we were part of a Renaissance fair to explain our strange clothing and why we all smelled of smoke. I finally convinced them the poisoning was a mistake, that she had been trying to cook some plants she found in the woods."

"Where's Jacob? Did he leave us again?" Gracie tried to sound casual, but her voice cracked on the last words. She picked ash from beneath her fingernail.

Mom shook her head. "He's in the waiting room. He's been worried about you, but he said he didn't know if you'd want to see him."

"I know he's sorry," Gracie said. "But he still shouldn't have left us."

"No, he shouldn't have." Mom was silent for a moment. "But I think you should know the whole story before you make up your mind about him."

"A story?"

"Bad choice of words. The facts, I mean." Mom smiled thinly and took a deep breath. "For the first few months after we escaped Bondoff, when you were a baby, Jacob didn't leave. He stayed nearby." Mom's eyes met Gracie's; guilt played on her face. "I was still so hurt and angry over what he'd done, and one day we had an argument. I told him I never wanted to see him again." She folded her hands in her lap.

"That's not your fault; everyone says things they don't mean. Jacob still *chose* to leave."

"Perhaps. But I still wonder what would've happened if I'd never said those words."

Gracie thought back to when she'd confronted Jacob in Bondoff. It was a relief to tell him how she felt, but her anger had been followed the way it always was, with a story glimmer, the rage, the vision of Cassandra. "If I don't want to see him now, do you think that's the villain part of me being mad?"

"Being angry doesn't make you a villain, Gracie. Anger can help you stand up for yourself, do the things you need to. It can be a good thing, if you control it rather than letting it control you."

"What do you think I should do?"

Mom shook her head. "It's up to you whether you want to give Jacob a chance. You have to do what's best for *you*. If you decide you don't want to see him, that won't make you a villain."

"Do you forgive Jacob?"

Mom bit her lip. "I don't know. Not yet, maybe, but I think I'd like to give him a chance. I can see how much he cares for us. I think he really is a different person now."

There was a knock at the door, and Walter poked his head in. "Can I talk to Gracie?"

Mom stood up. "I need to go tell Jacob that Gracie's awake, anyway. He was worried that she hadn't woken up yet."

Gracie stared at the blanket. She still didn't think she could meet Walter's eyes. She wished Mom wouldn't leave her alone with him, but she knew she had to face him eventually, even if he'd probably never forgive her for what she'd done. At least he was willing to talk to her, though. She watched her mother's back as she left. "Mom, wait!"

"Hmm?" Mom turned in the doorway.

"You can tell Jacob if he comes to see me, I'll talk to him."

Mom smiled. "I think he'll be very happy to hear that."

Walter waited for Mom to leave before he spoke. "You tried to kill me." Walter sat on the edge of Gracie's bed, shoving his glasses up on his nose. Gracie couldn't read his blank expression, but his voice sounded more interested than angry.

"I'm sorry, Walter." Gracie twisted the blanket between her fingers. "I didn't mean to. Everything was so different in the story."

"I suppose this means we're not friends anymore."

Gracie tugged at her hospital bracelet. "I don't blame you."

"Now I know why my parents got so upset when you hit me. They probably worried you'd light me on fire next."

"Yeah, I guess." Gracie bit her lip. "I did the right thing in the end, though!" The words came out in a rush. She'd heard these words before. It was what Jacob had said, too. "Doesn't that count for something? I tried to kill you, but I saved you too. I didn't want to hurt you, not really."

Walter snorted.

"What's so funny?" Gracie stiffened.

"The thought of you as the villain in a story!" Walter smirked. "You are so not villain material."

"What's that supposed to mean?"

"What kind of a villain runs in and rescues her victims?"

Gracie glared at him. Why did Walter have to be so irritating? Right when Gracie was trying to apologize for what she'd done, too. She realized with a jolt that she was getting angry, and yet there was no scent of smoke, no hint of a story glimmer coming on. This made her so happy she laughed out loud. "I thought you didn't read stories anyway? What do you know about villains?"

Walter shrugged. "I was talking to Gertrude Winters earlier, and I got to thinking. Stories could be really cool if we could study them scientifically. Like how could a place like Bondoff exist? And what if there are more worlds like it? Wouldn't that be fascinating? What if every story ever written is a world in another dimension, waiting for us to find it?"

"Did you forget how awful it was in the story we were just in?"

"That was the most exciting thing that's ever happened to me! I'm probably the first scientist ever to visit another dimension. I thought you of all people would understand, the way you're always talking about stories."

Gracie thought about this. "I think I want to write my own story for a while."

Walter grinned. "Just so long as you don't come after me again."

Gracie felt her cheeks grow warm. "So can we still be friends?"

Walter was silent for a moment. "Don't you think that if we are both people created by Gertrude Winters, that kind of makes us related? Like we must be family in some weird way? Some kind of story-cousins or something?"

Gracie nodded. "Probably."

Walter squeezed her hand. "Speaking of Gertrude Winters," he said. "She wanted to talk to you. I told her I'd tell you when you woke up."

ღღ

Gracie and Walter padded down the hall to Gertrude's room. She was asleep. Her face was thin, but at least it was clean now. The nurses must have washed her hair. She looked peaceful. Gracie wasn't sure if she should wake her, but then Gertrude's eyes snapped open. "I've been waiting for you to come see me," she said. "I wanted to talk to you about Cassandra."

Gracie and Walter pulled chairs up beside the bed. "What about her?" Gracie said.

"You said back at the castle that Cassandra never had a chance to be other than how I'd written her. I can't help feeling that this is all my fault—I made her the way she was." Gertrude Winters rubbed sleep from her eyes. "Where's the book?" she said.

"What?" Gracie said.

"I asked your mother if I could examine the Vademecum. I never got to look at it much back in Bondoff, and it's so fascinating to see an object I dreamed up for a story come to life in the real world. I was holding it when I fell asleep."

"Maybe my mom took it when you were sleeping," Gracie said. "We can ask her when she comes back."

Gertrude Winters sighed. "Maybe. She didn't seem too happy to give it to me. I don't think your mother likes me very much."

"Never mind about that," Gracie said. "What did you want to tell me about Cassandra?"

Gertrude adjusted her pillows so she was sitting up straighter. "I was thinking that if we really want to give Cassandra a chance at a new life here, maybe I should take her to live with me. At least for a little while until she gets on her feet. I could get to know her a bit—she always was one of my favorite characters, and she is so like myself that I think we could get along really well. She's almost like a daughter to me, in a way."

Gracie thought back to the conversation she'd had with Gertrude in the tower. "What about your real daughter?"

Gertrude leaned her head back on the pillow and closed her eyes. "I telephoned her this morning. I said what I should have, and she asked for some time to think. In the meantime, while I wait for her response, I will have Cassandra."

"You're not mad that she locked you in a tower?" Walter said.

Gertrude waved her hand dismissively. "It's the way I wrote her. I told Gracie already, the villains are some of the most intriguing characters. We're all a mixture of good and bad. And Cassandra's no threat to me anymore, not without the Vademecum."

A nurse entered with a tray of food. "Time to eat," she told Gertrude. "You need to keep your strength up." She turned to Gracie. "I left your tray in your room, but I can bring it in here if you like, so you can eat together."

"That's okay," Gracie said. "I'm going back to my room anyway. My mom will be looking for me."

"Did you see the book I had with me?" Gertrude Winters said to the nurse. "I had it when I fell asleep."

"A woman came in and took it while you were sleeping," the nurse said. "She said it was hers."

"What woman?" Gracie said. "My mom?"

The nurse shook her head. "No, that other woman you all came in with. The dark-haired one. She was a bit rude, to be honest. She went storming out of here, even though the doctors told her she wasn't well enough to leave yet."

"Where is she?" Gracie said.

The nurse shrugged. "No idea."

ಞ

They loaded into two cars: Jacob, Mom, and Gracie in the truck, pulling Jacob's camper behind them; and Walter, his parents, and Gertrude Winters following in the other car. Gracie looked out the window as they drove.

"It's all my fault," she said. "If I hadn't tried to save Cassandra, she wouldn't have stolen the book back, and we wouldn't be running again."

"You did the right thing," Mom said. "You were kind. You showed empathy for another person. You should never be ashamed of that."

Gracie leaned her forehead against the glass.

"We'll start over," Jacob said. "Together, in a new place. We won't let Cassandra find us this time, and who knows if she'll even be looking for us after everything that happened. Cassandra isn't someone who would risk her life too many times, not after how close she was to dying last time she brought us back into the story."

"Maybe," Gracie said. She looked over her shoulder at Walter's parents' car behind them. Walter rode in the back beside Gertrude Winters. Gertrude had wanted to go into hiding with them because she was afraid Cassandra would come looking for her, and because she said she wanted to get to know Gracie, Walter, and their parents better. She said they felt like family.

"It almost feels like before," Mom said. "When we left Bondoff twelve years ago."

Gracie thought about this. It was true that they were running again, and Cassandra was loose and had the Vademecum. But Jacob was staying with them this time. And even if Gracie still feared Cassandra, she no longer wondered about Gertrude's story. She would never again worry over what was written about her. "It's not at all the same as last time."

"I just meant it's like we're getting a second chance to begin again," Mom said, and Jacob patted her hand.

Mom and Jacob exchanged a look. Gracie didn't know if they would ever get back together, but at least they were friends. Even if they'd made mistakes, she knew both of them loved her and cared about her. Both of them had tried to protect her, in their separate ways.

Gracie rested her head on Mom's shoulder. She was content here with Mom and Jacob. She didn't know where they would end up, or what the future held for them, but somehow not knowing who she was or who she would be was okay with her. She was simply Gracie, her future unwritten.

AUTHOR Q&A

Q: *Unwritten* explores the common theme of good versus evil and gives it a twist. Can you talk about why you chose to do that?

Tara: I've been really concerned lately about this tendency we have, especially in our social media-focused culture, where our mistakes can immediately be made public, to label others as either "completely good" or "completely bad." We all slip up and do bad things, and in the end, all we can hope to do is learn from those mistakes and move forward. People are complex, and we all have bad and good inside of us. I hope *Unwritten* can inspire readers to have compassion for others when they make mistakes and be open to giving people second chances.

Q: Is *Unwritten* inspired by any specific fairy tales or other fantasy books?

Tara: Definitely! My earlier drafts were filled with even more fairy tale elements than the final book (my first draft even contained a very long section where Gracie and Walter go inside the tale "Sleeping Beauty"!). I read books like Jack Zipes's *Why Fairy Tales Stick* and Bruno Bettelheim's *The Uses of Enchantment*, which explore why we're so drawn to fairy tale elements like wicked stepmothers, magical transformations, potions, and children wandering around in forests. Of course, in the original fairy tales, the nature of good and evil isn't so cut and dry either. Zipes and Bettelheim's work is fascinating, and I know I was especially influenced by Zipes's thoughts on wicked stepmothers as I was creating Cassandra's character.

I also read books like *Inkheart*, with premises similar to mine, that I used as "mentor texts" as I was writing, both to see how they had handled the world-building involved in creating a "story-within-a-story" fantasy world and to make sure I wasn't doing anything too similar to what those authors had already done.

Q: Where do you find your inspiration to write?

Tara: From reading! I am first and foremost a reader, even more than I am a writer. It's my absolute favorite thing to do. Reading good stories always leaves me feeling inspired to write my own. On days when I am struggling with what to write, I know if I sit down and read one of my favorite books for an hour, I'll be scribbling in my notebook before the hour is up!

Q: What's the best thing about being a writer?

Tara: The friends I've made because of my writing. It was only when I started graduate school and met other writers for the first time that I realized there were other people like me in the world: people who spend their days reading stories and dreaming up imaginary characters. The people in my workshop group are some of my dearest friends, and we are constantly supporting one another (not to mention chatting for hours about storytelling!). They are the best.

Q: What's your advice for aspiring writers?

Tara: Read a lot, write a lot, and keep at it. One of my writing teachers once told me something along the lines of: "I've taught a lot of great writers over the years, and in the end, it wasn't the most talented ones who published books. It was the ones who worked the hardest and were the most persistent." That advice has always stuck with me. I can't control how much talent I have, or the publishing market, or a lot of other things about my writing career, but I can control how hard I work.

Q: Who is your favorite *Unwritten* character and why?

Tara: Definitely Gracie. Though she has her flaws, she's also passionate, determined, and loyal. And like Gertrude Winters, I always find the most flawed characters the most interesting.

Q: Are you like Gracie in any way?

Tara: Yes, probably more than I'd like to admit! As my friends and family could tell you, like Gracie, I can be stubborn and a bit hard-headed.

Q: Is there more to Gracie's story? Do you have any future plans for the characters from Bondoff?

Tara: I think there is definitely more to Gracie's story! I think about her all the time and have actually begun writing some scenes that take place after the events of *Unwritten* are over. I've also been daydreaming quite a bit about Gertrude Winters and the other stories she's written.

Q: No one is quite what they seem in *Unwritten* and there are quite a few twists and turns. Did you always have a clear plan for how it was going to work out or were there surprises for you too?

Tara: No, I did not have a clear plan at all! I think I was as surprised by the twists and turns as anyone. When I'm writing my first drafts, I usually don't make an outline ahead of time because I need to spend some time getting to know my characters. Otherwise I feel like I am forcing my characters to say and do things that don't feel natural for them. It took me a few drafts to really get a sense of Gracie and who she is. Cassandra and Gertrude Winters were also tough characters to get to know, and it was only after quite a bit of revision that I had their motivations sorted out. Once I knew who my characters were and what they wanted, developing the plot became a lot easier.

Q: What was your favorite fairy tale when you were a kid?

Tara: Cinderella. And then later I fell in love with Frances Hodgson Burnett's novel, *A Little Princess*, which draws on elements of the Cinderella tale. My friends and I would play dress-up and argue over who got to be the servant. I'm not sure why we were so drawn to this role. I think it likely had something to do with the fact that we liked the idea of transformation, of starting out in a downtrodden role, and then later showing people our true selves. I think this is something every kid dreams about in different ways. As kids, we often feel a bit unseen and invalidated by adults, and we all wait for the day when we will grow up and show the world how great we are.

ACKNOWLEDGMENTS

Any novel is a collaborative effort, and I could not have written this one without the help of many kind, thoughtful, and supportive people. Jill Bixel, my critique partner, who not only cheered me on through more drafts than I can count, but who also closely read each draft and gently pointed out what still needed work. This novel would not be the same without her insights. Sarah Aronson, who helped me in the beginning stages of this novel and steered me in the right direction, pushing me to dig deeper into Gracie's character and the novel's main conflicts. Her mentorship made me not only a better writer, but a better teacher as well. The members of the RCC, my wonderful workshop group—Patti Edgar, Michelle Barker, Kate Lum, and Kim McCullough—not only did they offer invaluable advice and patiently read many drafts of this, but their example pushes me every day to be a better writer. Catherine Young, who read drafts, offered feedback, and believed in this book even when I didn't.

I've had many wonderful writing teachers who shaped my development as a writer, especially Dean Karpowicz, who first empowered me to believe I could be a writer (and taught me to edit); Gail-Anderson Dargatz, who changed the way I thought about writing fiction; and Maggie DeVries, who introduced me to the joys of writing for children. I would not have written this book had I not been lucky enough to study under them.

I want to thank everyone at Jolly Fish, especially Mari Kesselring, who championed this book and helped make it better—I am so lucky to have such a smart and supportive editor. (She is also always right.) Jake Slavik, for the cover design, and Jomike Tejido, for his beautiful illustration. I am so in awe of the stunning cover they created for my book. Megan Naidl, for all her hard work with marketing and communications.

My family: Samantha Gilboy, my amazing daughter, who was excited about this book from the beginning and helped with many impromptu brainstorming sessions. Kurt Gilboy, my husband, who not only made sure all the bills got paid while I was writing but is always willing to listen to me ramble about fictional characters. Biscuit, who cuddled on my lap while I wrote this book and went on the long walks where I puzzled out plot problems. Julie Newbury: you introduced me to reading, you bought my childhood writing notebooks, read all my stories, finished this novel in one sitting, and always *always* believed in me. How can I ever repay you?

ABOUT THE AUTHOR

Tara Gilboy holds a Master of Fine Arts in Creative Writing from the University of British Columbia, where she specialized in writing for children and young adults. She teaches creative writing for San Diego Continuing Education and lives in southern California with her husband, daughter, and dog, Biscuit.

WITHDRAWN